...adn't all

...g with shocking clarity, and without a word for her he turned from the room and bounded up the stairs.

'Larenzo—' She hurried after him, one arm flung towards him in desperate supplication. 'Larenzo, please, don't—'

He could hear the child crying, the voice pitiful and plaintive.

'Mama. Mama.'

He threw open the door and came to a complete and stunned halt as he saw the baby standing in her cot, chubby fists gripping the rail, cherubic face screwed up and wet with tears.

And Larenzo knew. He would have known just by looking at the child, with her ink-dark hair and large grey eyes, the cleft in her chin. He turned to Emma, who was gazing at him with undisguised panic.

'When,' he asked in ... ...ere you going to tell me a...

One Night With Consequences

When one night...leads to pregnancy!

When succumbing to a night of unbridled desire
it's impossible to think past the morning after!

But, with the sheets barely settled, that little blue line
appears on the pregnancy test and it doesn't take long
to realise that one night of white-hot passion
has turned into a lifetime of consequences!

Only one question remains:

How do you tell a man you've just met
that you're about to share more than just his bed?

Find out in:

Nine Months to Redeem Him by Jennie Lucas
January 2015

Prince Nadir's Secret Heir by Michelle Conder
March 2015

Carrying the Greek's Heir by Sharon Kendrick
April 2015

Married for Amari's Heir by Maisey Yates
July 2015

Bound by the Billionaire's Baby by Cathy Williams
July 2015

From One Night to Wife by Rachael Thomas
September 2015

Her Nine Month Confession by Kim Lawrence
September 2015

Look for more *One Night With Consequences*
coming soon!

If you missed any of these fabulous stories,
they can be found at millsandboon.co.uk

LARENZO'S
CHRISTMAS BABY

BY
KATE HEWITT

Published in Great Britain 2015
by Mills & Boon, an imprint of Harlequin (UK) Limited,
Eton House, 18-24 Paradise Road, Richmond, Surrey, TW9 1SR

© 2015 Kate Hewitt

ISBN: 978-0-263-24931-6

Printed and bound in Spain
by CPI, Barcelona

After spending three years as a die-hard New Yorker, **Kate Hewitt** now lives in a small village in the English Lake District with her husband, their five children and a golden retriever. In addition to writing intensely emotional stories she loves reading, baking, and playing chess with her son—she has yet to win against him, but she continues to try.

Learn more about Kate at www.kate-hewitt.com.

Books by Kate Hewitt

Mills & Boon Modern Romance

Kholodov's Last Mistress
The Undoing of de Luca

The Marakaios Brides

The Marakaios Marriage
The Marakaios Baby

The Chatsfield

Virgin's Sweet Rebellion

Rivals to the Crown of Kadar

Captured by the Sheikh
Commanded by the Sheikh

The Diomedi Heirs

The Prince She Never Knew
A Queen for the Taking?

The Bryants: Powerful & Proud

Beneath the Veil of Paradise
In the Heat of the Spotlight
His Brand of Passion

The Power of Redemption

The Darkest of Secrets
The Husband She Never Knew

Visit the Author Profile page
at millsandboon.co.uk for more titles.

CHAPTER ONE

THE SOUND OF the car door slamming echoed through the still night. Emma Leighton looked up from the book she'd been reading in surprise; as housekeeper of Larenzo Cavelli's isolated retreat in the mountains of Sicily, she hadn't been expecting anyone. Larenzo was in Rome on business, and no one came to the villa perched high above Sicily's dusty hill towns and villages. Her employer liked his privacy.

She heard brisk footsteps on the stone path that led to the villa's front door, an enormous thing of solid oak banded with iron. She tensed, waiting for a knock; the villa had an elaborate security system with a numbered code that was only known by her and Larenzo, and the door was locked, as Larenzo always insisted.

She held her breath as she heard the creak of the door opening and then the beep of buttons being pressed, followed by a longer beeping indicating the security system had been deactivated. As her heart did a queasy little flip, Emma tossed her book aside and rose from her chair. Larenzo never came back early or unexpectedly. He always texted her, to make sure she had everything ready for his arrival: his bed made with freshly ironed sheets, the fridge stocked, the pool heated. But if it *wasn't* him…who was it?

She heard footsteps coming closer, a heavy, deliberate tread, and then a figure, tall and rangy, appeared in the doorway.

'*Larenzo*—' Emma pressed one hand to her chest as she let out a shaky laugh of relief. 'You scared me. I wasn't expecting you.'

'I wasn't expecting to come here.' He stepped into the spacious sitting room of the villa, and as the lamplight washed over his face Emma sucked in a shocked breath. Larenzo's skin looked grey, and there were deep shadows under his eyes. His hair was rumpled, as if he'd driven his hand through the ink-dark strands.

'Are you—are you all right?'

His mouth twisted in a grim smile. 'Why, do I not look all right?'

'No, not really.' She tried to lighten her words with a smile, but she really was alarmed. In the nine months she'd been Larenzo's housekeeper, she'd never seen him look like this, not just tired or haggard, but as if the life force that was so much a part of who he was, that restless, rangy energy and charisma, had drained away.

'Are you ill?' she asked. 'I can get you something…'

'No. Not ill.' He let out a hollow laugh. 'But clearly I must look terrible.'

'Well, as a matter of fact, yes, you do.'

'Thank you for your honesty.'

'Sorry—'

'Don't be. I can't bear lies.' A sudden, savage note had entered his voice, making Emma blink. Larenzo crossed the room to the liquor cabinet in the corner. 'I need a drink.'

She watched as he poured himself a large measure of whisky and then tossed it back in one burning swallow. His back was to her, the silk of his suit jacket straining against his shoulders and sinewy back. He was an attractive man, a beautiful man even, with his blue-black hair and piercing grey eyes, his tall, powerful body always encased in three-thousand-euro suits.

Emma had admired his form the way you admired Michelangelo's *David*, as a work of art. She had decided when she'd taken this job that she wasn't going to make the mistake of developing some schoolgirl crush on her boss. Larenzo Cavelli was out of her league. Way, way out of her league. And, if the tabloids were true, he had a different woman on his arm and in his bed every week.

'I wasn't expecting you until the end of the month,' she said.

'I had a change of plans.' He took out the stopper in the crystal decanter of whisky and poured himself another healthy measure. 'Obviously.'

She didn't press the point, because, while they'd developed a fairly amicable working relationship over the last nine months, he was still her boss. She couldn't actually say she *knew* Larenzo Cavelli. Since she'd taken the job as housekeeper he'd come to the villa only three times, never more than for a couple of days. He mostly lived in Rome, where he kept an apartment, or travelled for work as CEO of Cavelli Enterprises.

'Very well,' she finally said. 'Will you be staying long?'

He drained his glass for a second time. 'Probably not.'

'Well, the night at least,' she answered briskly. She didn't know what was going on with Larenzo, whether it was a business deal gone bust or a love affair gone bad, or something else entirely, but she could still do her job. 'The sheets on your bed are clean. I'll go switch the heating on for the pool.'

'Don't bother,' Larenzo answered. He put his empty glass on the table with a clink. 'There's no need.'

'It's no trouble,' Emma protested, and Larenzo shrugged, his back to her.

'Fine. Maybe I'll have one last swim.'

His words replayed through her mind as she left him and walked through the spacious, silent rooms of the villa to the back door that led to a brick terrace overlooking the mountains, a teardrop-shaped pool as its impressive centrepiece. *One last swim.* Was he planning on leaving, on selling the villa?

Emma gazed out at the Nebrodi mountains and shivered slightly, for the air still held a pine-scented chill.

All was quiet save for the rustling of the wind high up in the trees. Larenzo's villa was remote, miles from the nearest market town, Troina; in the daylight Emma could see its terracotta-tiled houses and shops nestled in the valley below. She went there several times a week to shop and socialise; she had a couple of friends amidst the Sicilian shopkeepers and matrons.

If Larenzo was planning on selling the villa, she'd miss living here. She never stayed anywhere long, and she would have probably started feeling restless in a few months anyway, but… She glanced once more at the night-cloaked hills and valleys, the mellow stone of the villa perched on its hill gleaming in the moonlight. She liked living here. It was peaceful, with plenty of subjects to photograph. She'd be sad to leave, if it came to that.

But maybe Larenzo just meant a swim before he left for Rome again. She switched on the heating and then turned to go inside; as she turned a shadowy form loomed up in front of her and her breath came out in a short gasp. She must have swayed or stumbled a little, for Larenzo put his hands on her shoulders to steady her.

They stood like that for a moment in the doorway, his strong hands curling around her shoulders so she could feel the warmth of his palms through the thin cotton of her T-shirt, and how her heart pounded beneath it. She didn't think he'd ever actually touched her before.

She moved one way, and he moved another, so it was almost as if they were engaged in a struggle or an awkward dance. Then Larenzo dropped his hands from her shoulders and stepped back.

'Scusi.'

'My fault,' she murmured, her heart still thudding, and moved quickly through the kitchen to flick on the lights. Bathed in a bright electric glow, things felt more normal, even if she could still feel the imprint of his hands on her shoulders, so warm and strong. 'So.' She turned to him with a quick smile, a brisk look. 'Have you eaten? I can make you something.'

He looked as if he was about to refuse, and then he shrugged. 'Why not? I'll go change while you cook.'

'What would you like to eat?'

Another shrug as he turned away. 'Whatever you make will be fine.'

She watched him disappear down the hallway, her lips pursed in an uncertain frown. She'd never seen Larenzo like this. Not that they'd actually had that much conversation, beyond discussing pool maintenance and house repairs. But even when talking about such mundane matters, Larenzo Cavelli had exuded a compelling charisma and energy, a life force. He was a man who, when entering a room, made everyone turn and take notice. Men tried to suppress their envy, and women undressed him with their eyes. Emma counted herself as wilfully immune to the man's magnetic vitality, but its absence now made her uneasy.

Her frown deepening, Emma opened the fridge and stared at the few items inside. She always did a big shop right before Larenzo arrived; she bought all the ingredients for gourmet meals for one and made them for him to eat alone, usually out on the terrace overlooking the mountains.

Now she glanced askance at the half-dozen eggs, a few slices of pancetta and the end of a wedge of cheese that comprised the entire contents of the fridge. With a sigh she took it all out. A bacon and cheese omelette it was.

She was just sliding it onto a plate when Larenzo came downstairs, dressed now in faded jeans and a grey T-shirt, his hair damp and spiky from a shower. She'd seen him casually dressed before, many times, but for some reason now, perhaps because of how different Larenzo seemed, her heart gave a weird little flip and she felt awareness shiver over her skin. Clearly he still possessed some of that charisma and vitality, for she felt the force of it now.

'Sorry it's just an omelette,' she said. 'I'll do a big shop tomorrow.'

'That won't be necessary.'

'But—'

"Aren't you going to join me?' He arched an eyebrow, nodding towards the single plate she'd laid out, a challenge simmering in his eyes.

In the handful of times he'd been at the villa, Larenzo had never asked her to eat with him. The two of them alone on the terrace would have been awkward, intimate, and Emma happily ate leftovers in the kitchen, one of her photography books propped against the salt and pepper shakers.

'Um…I've already eaten,' she said after a second's pause. It had to be past ten o'clock at night.

'Come have a glass of wine. I don't feel like being alone.'

Was that a command? Emma shrugged her assent; she wouldn't mind a glass of wine, and perhaps Larenzo would tell her what was going on.

'Okay,' she said, and she fetched two glasses while Larenzo selected a bottle of red wine from the rack above the sink.

While Larenzo took his plate of eggs out to the terrace, Emma retrieved her sweater from the sitting room, slipping her arms through the sleeves as she stepped outside. The moon was high and full above the pine-blanketed hills, the Nebrodi range's highest peak, Mount Soro, piercing the night sky. Larenzo was already seated at a table overlooking the pool, the water glimmering in the moonlight, but he rose as Emma came forward with the two glasses and proffered the bottle of wine. She nodded her assent and sat down while he poured.

'This is very civilised,' she said as she accepted the glass.

'Yes, isn't it?' Larenzo answered. 'Well, let's enjoy it while we can.' He raised his glass in a toast and Emma lifted hers as well before taking a sip. The wine was rich and velvety-smooth, clearly expensive, but she put her glass down after one sip and gave her boss as direct a look as she could.

'You're sure everything is all right?'

'As right as it can be,' Larenzo answered, taking a sip of wine.

'What does that mean?'

He set his glass down and stretched his legs out in front of him. 'Exactly that. But I don't want to talk about myself, not tonight. For a few hours I'd just like to forget.'

Forget what? Emma wondered, but clearly Larenzo didn't want her to ask.

'You've been my housekeeper for nearly a year and I don't really know the first thing about you,' he continued, and Emma stared at him in surprise.

'You want to talk about *me*?'

'Why not?'

'Because…well, because you've never expressed an interest in knowing anything about me before. And actually, I'm quite a boring person.'

He smiled, his teeth gleaming in the darkness. 'Let me be the judge of that.'

Emma shook her head slowly. This evening was becoming almost surreal. 'What do you want to know?'

'Where did you grow up?'

An innocuous enough question, she supposed. 'Everywhere, really. I was a diplomat's kid.'

'I think I remember you mentioning that in your interview.' He'd interviewed her in Rome, where she'd been working as a chambermaid in a hotel, just one in a string of jobs she'd had as she moved from city to city, exploring the world and taking photographs.

'And you haven't minded being stuck up here in the hills of Sicily?' he asked, his wine glass raised to his lips. 'All by yourself?'

She shrugged. 'I'm used to being on my own.' And she preferred it that way. No ties, no obligations, no disappointments. The occasional bout of loneliness was not too high a price to pay for that kind of freedom.

'Even so.'

'You obviously like it,' she pointed out. 'Since you own this place.'

'Yes, but I travel and spend time in cities. I'm not up here all the time.'

'Well, as I said, I like it.' For now, anyway. She never remained anywhere for too long, always preferring to move on, to find new experiences, and from the sceptical look on Larenzo's face he seemed to guess a bit of her natural wanderlust.

'Have you met anyone up here?' he asked. 'Made friends?'

'A few people down in Troina.'

'That's something, I suppose. What do you do for fun up here?'

Emma shrugged. 'Walk. Swim. Read. I'm easily entertained, fortunately.'

'Yes.' He gazed out at the mountains and Emma had

the sense he was thinking about something else, something painful.

'But it's not the kind of job you'd stay in for ever,' he said at last.

'Are you trying to get rid of me?' she asked lightly. She'd meant it as a joke but Larenzo took the question seriously.

'No, definitely not. But if something were to happen…' He trailed off, his gaze still on the hills, and Emma set down her wine glass.

'Larenzo, are you thinking of selling this place?'

'Not selling it, no.'

'But something,' she pressed. 'What's going on, really? Do I need to start looking for another job?'

He let out a long, low breath and raked his hands through his hair. 'Whatever happens, I'll make sure to give you a good reference.'

'What are you talking about, whatever happens?' Emma shook her head. 'I don't understand you.'

'I know, and I don't want to explain it now. It will all become clear soon enough.' He nodded towards the pool. 'How about a swim?'

'A *swim*?' Emma glanced at the pool, the water glimmering in the moonlight. 'It's a bit cold for me.'

'Not for me,' he said, and she watched in amazement as he stripped off his shirt and jeans and, clad only in his boxer shorts, dived into the pool.

The splash echoed through the still air and Emma watched, shivering slightly, as Larenzo swam the length of the pool before surfacing and slicking back the wet hair from his face.

'Come in,' he called. 'The water's lovely.'

Emma shook her head. 'I only just turned the heating on. It's got to be freezing.'

'Even so.' He arched an eyebrow, his mouth curling in a smile that was pure temptation. Emma's gaze was inexorably drawn to his bare chest, all lean, rippling muscle, his bronzed skin beaded with water. 'Dare you.'

Emma hadn't thought this evening could get any more surreal. But swimming with her boss in a freezing pool?

'Come on, Emma.' He held out his hand. 'Just jump in.' Heat simmered in his eyes and she felt an answering stab of lust through her middle.

This was so foolish, so dangerous, and yet…the sight of Larenzo in the pool, nearly naked with moonlight streaming over his body and droplets of water twinkling like diamonds on his bronzed skin, was hard to resist. And already this evening felt separate from reality, a time apart.

'Chicken?' he taunted, his eyes and teeth glinting in the darkness, and Emma laughed.

'You really want to get me in that pool.'

'I want someone to swim with.'

Excitement licked through her veins. She didn't think Larenzo was coming on to her; he never had before. And yet…

'Fine,' she said, and, shrugging off her sweater, she dived fully clothed into the deep end.

She surfaced, sucking in a hard breath, because the water really was cold. 'And now I'm getting out,' she told him as she trod water. 'It's as freezing as I thought it would be.'

'I didn't think you'd do it,' he said, laughter threading his voice, and Emma was glad that she'd managed to distract him from whatever had been bothering him, even if she got hypothermia in the process.

'You thought wrong,' she said, and swam towards the edge of the pool. With her wet clothes weighing her down it was hard to haul herself up on the pool's edge.

And then she felt Larenzo behind her, his hands on her shoulders, the strength and heat of him just inches from her back. She sucked in a shocked breath as he slid his hands to her waist and helped her up.

She flopped inelegantly on the side of the pool and then scrambled to her knees, amazed at how much that one little touch had affected her. She shivered, for with her soaked clothes the night air now felt icy.

'Here.' Larenzo hauled himself up and went to the heated cupboard for several towels. 'Wrap yourself up.'

'I should really change,' she said. She glanced down at herself and saw that her T-shirt was sticking to her skin, revealing even the floral pattern on her bra, her nipples peaked from the cold. 'Thanks,' she muttered, and clutched the towel to her chest.

Larenzo's gaze hadn't dropped to her chest, but his mouth curved all the same and again Emma felt another kick of excitement. She retreated back to the table, the towel still clutched to her chest.

'I should go to bed.'

'Don't go quite yet,' Larenzo answered. He slung the towel over his shoulders and sat down across from her, pouring them both more wine. Emma eyed the full glass and Larenzo's bare chest, his perfectly formed pecs flexing as he moved, and felt as if she'd just jumped into the deep end of an entirely different kind of pool.

'I'm freezing—' she began and he nodded towards the cupboard.

'There are towelling robes in there. Change out of your wet things. I don't want you catching cold.'

'Larenzo…' Emma began, although she didn't know what she was going to say. Why was she protesting so much, anyway? Chatting in the moonlight with a devastatingly attractive man was no hardship. And it wasn't as if Larenzo was going to make a move. He might have dared her to jump in the pool, but she was pretty sure her boss didn't mix business with pleasure.

Even if she wanted him to…

'Fine,' she said, and retreated to the towelling cupboard.

With the door serving as a screen between her and Larenzo, she tugged off her wet clothes and wrapped herself in the heated dressing gown. The sleeves hung past her hands and the sash trailed the ground, but at least she was warm again. She doubted she'd provide any sort of temptation to Larenzo now.

'Tell me your favourite place you lived in as a child,' Larenzo commanded as she sat down across from him and picked up her wine glass—he'd filled it again, while she'd been changing.

Emma considered for a moment. Answering questions, at least, kept her from gawping at Larenzo's chest. Why on earth she was feeling this unwelcome attraction for him now, she had no idea. Perhaps it was simply the strangeness of the evening, his unexpected arrival, his demand for her company. 'Krakow, I suppose,' she said finally. 'I spent two years there when I was ten. It's a beautiful city.' And those years had been the last ones where she'd felt part of a family, before her mother had announced her decision to leave. But she didn't want to think, much less talk, about that. 'Where did you grow up?' she asked, and Larenzo swirled the wine in his glass, his expression hardening slightly as he gazed down into its ruby depths.

'Palermo.'

'Hence the villa in Sicily, I suppose.'

'It is my home.'

'But you live most of the time in Rome.'

'Cavelli Enterprises is headquartered there.' He paused, his shuttered gaze on the darkened mountains, the moon casting a lambent glow over the wooded hills. 'In any case, I never much liked Palermo.'

'Why not?'

He pressed his lips together. 'Too many hard memories.'

He didn't seem inclined to say anything more, and Emma eyed him curiously, wondering at this enigmatic man who clearly had secrets she'd never even guessed at before.

Larenzo gazed round the terrace, the patio furniture now no more than shadowy shapes in the darkness, and then turned to look once more at the mountains. 'I'll miss it here,' he said, so quietly Emma almost didn't hear him.

'So you are thinking of leaving,' she said, and Larenzo didn't answer for a long moment.

'Not thinking of it, no,' he said, and then seemed to shake off his weary mood, his gaze snapping back to her. 'Thank you, Emma, for the food and also for your company. You've done more for me than you could possibly know.'

Emma stared at him helplessly. 'If there's anything else I can do…'

To her shock he touched her cheek with his hand, his fingers cool against her flushed face. *'Bellissima,'* he whispered, and the endearment stole right through her. 'No,' he said, and dropped his hand from her face. 'You've done enough. Thank you.' And then, taking his plate and his glass, he rose from his chair and left her sitting on the terrace alone.

Emma sat there for a few moments, shivering a little in the chilly air despite the dressing gown. She wished she could have comforted Larenzo somehow, but she had no idea what was going on, and she wasn't sure he'd welcome her sympathy anyway. He was a proud, hard man, caught in a moment of weakness. He'd probably regret their whole conversation tomorrow.

Sighing, she took the wine bottle and glasses from the table and headed inside. Larenzo had already gone upstairs; the lights were off, the house locked up. After rinsing out the dishes and switching on the dishwasher Emma went upstairs as well.

She paused for a moment on the landing; Larenzo's

master bedroom was to the right, her own smaller room the last on the left. She heard nothing but the wind high up in the trees, and she couldn't see any light underneath Larenzo's doorway. Even so she had a mad urge to knock on his door, to say something. But what? They didn't have that kind of relationship, not remotely, and knocking on Larenzo's bedroom door, seeing him answer it with his hair rumpled and damp, his chest still bare…

No. That was taking this strange evening a step too far.

Still she hesitated, glancing towards his doorway, and then with a sigh she turned and went to her own bedroom, closing the door behind her.

CHAPTER TWO

HE COULDN'T SLEEP. Hardly a surprise, considering all that had happened in the last few days. Larenzo stared gritty-eyed at the ceiling before, with a sigh, he sat up and swung his legs over the side of his bed.

All around him the house was still and silent. It was nearly two in the morning, and he wondered how long he had left. Would they come for him at dawn, or would they wait for the more civilised hour of eight or nine o'clock in the morning? Either way, it wouldn't be long. Bertrano had made sure of that.

Letting out another sigh at the thought of the man he'd considered as good as a father, Larenzo slipped from the bedroom and walked downstairs. The rooms of the villa were silent, dark, and empty, and he was loath to turn on a light and disturb the peacefulness. He could have stayed in Rome, but he'd hated the thought of simply waiting for the end, and he'd wanted to have a final farewell for the only place he could call a home. Bertrano would tell them where to find him; the police in Palermo had most likely already been alerted. He had a few hours at most.

And for those few hours he wanted simply to savour what he had. What Bertrano Raguso had given him, although Larenzo had worked hard for it. Ironic, really, that the man who had saved him would also destroy him. Fitting, perhaps.

He ran his hand along the silky-smooth ebony of the

grand piano in the music room; he'd bought it because he loved music, but he'd never found the time to learn to play. Now he never would. He played a few discordant notes, the sound echoing through the silent villa, before he moved onto the sitting room, stopping in front of the chessboard on a table by the window, its marble pieces set up for a game he would never play.

He picked up the king, fingering the smooth marble before he laid it down again. Bertrano had taught him how to play chess, and Larenzo had savoured the evenings they'd spent together, heads bent over a chessboard. Why had the man who had treated him like a son turned on him so suddenly? Betrayed him? Had it been a moment's panicked weakness? But no, it had gone on longer than that, perhaps even months, for Bertrano to lay the paper trail. How had Larenzo not known? Not even guessed?

He glanced at the pawns neatly lined up. In the end he'd served no more purpose than they did. With a sudden burst of helpless rage he struck the pawns, scattering them across the board with a clatter.

The realisation of all he was about to lose hit him then, with sickening force, and he dropped his face in his hands, driving his fingers through his hair, as a single sob racked his body.

Bertrano, how could you do this to me? I loved you. I thought of you as my father.

'Larenzo?'

He stiffened at the sound of Emma's uncertain voice, and then he lifted his face from his hands, turning to see her standing in the doorway of the sitting room. She was in her pyjamas, nothing more than boy shorts and a very thin T-shirt; Larenzo could see the outline of her small breasts and he felt an entirely inappropriate stab of lust, just as he had when he'd seen her soaked and dripping in the pool.

He hadn't spared much thought for his housekeeper before tonight, but now he envied her freedom, her ease.

'Couldn't you sleep?' she asked as she came into the room. She glanced at the scattered chess pieces, a silent question in her eyes.

'No, I couldn't.' He turned to the fireplace, where the kindling and logs were already laid for a fire. 'It's cold in here,' he said, and reached for a match to start the blaze. From behind him he could hear Emma righting the chess pieces.

When the fire was cheerily crackling in the hearth he turned to face her; she was touching the pawns he'd knocked over, her head bent, her hair swinging down to hide her face.

'Fancy a game?'

She looked up in surprise. 'What?'

He nodded towards the chessboard. 'Do you play?'

'I know the rules.'

'Well, then. It appears neither of us can sleep. Shall we play?'

'All right,' she said after a pause, and she sat down in one of the chairs as Larenzo sat in the other.

'White goes first,' he told her and she bit her lip, studying the board with a concentration so intense he found it endearing. Again he felt the powerful thrust of attraction. These few hours of enjoyment would be the last pleasure he had for a long while.

Finally she moved her piece, her slender fingers curling around the figure. She glanced up at him, a smile lurking in her eyes, playing with her lips. 'Why do I have a feeling you're going to crush me?'

'You can always live in hope,' he answered lightly, and moved his pawn.

She laughed, shaking her head. 'That would be foolish in the extreme.'

'Perhaps.' He liked watching her, seeing the way the

firelight played over her golden skin, how humour lit her golden-green eyes. He stretched out his legs and his foot brushed her ankle, sending another throb of desire through him.

He thought she felt something too, for her eyes widened and her body tensed briefly before she moved another piece on the board.

They played in silence for a few minutes, the tension spooling out between them. Larenzo brushed her foot again with his own, enjoying the silky slide of her skin. She sucked in a quick breath, her fingers trembling as she moved her rook.

'I'm four moves away from checkmate,' he told her, and she let out a shaky laugh.

'I knew this was going to happen.' She glanced up at him wryly and he held her gaze, felt the force of the attraction between them. He'd never considered his housekeeper as an object of desire before; employees had always been off limits, and he'd seen her so rarely. But tonight he craved that human connection, the last one that might ever be offered to him. To touch a woman, to give and receive pleasure...

Setting his jaw, Larenzo turned back towards the board. Making love with Emma tonight would be an entirely selfish act. He couldn't drag her down with him. It was bad enough that he was here at all.

He moved his bishop, and then stilled as he felt Emma's hand on his own, her skin cool and soft.

'Larenzo, I wish you'd tell me what's wrong.' He didn't answer, simply stared at her fingers on his. He stroked her palm with his thumb and she shivered in response but did not remove her hand.

'It doesn't matter,' he said in a low voice, and stroked her palm again. 'There's nothing you can do about it, and it's my own fault anyway.' For trusting someone he'd loved.

For believing someone could have pure motives. For being so bloody naive. So damn *stupid*.

'Are you sure I can't help?' Emma asked softly. She squeezed his fingers and Larenzo closed his eyes. Her touch was the sweetest torture he'd ever known. He thought of telling her the one way she could help, the one way she could make him forget what dawn would bring. He resisted. He could not be that selfish, not even on the threshold of his own destruction.

'No, I'm afraid not. No one can.'

Her gaze searched his face and then she rose from her chair. 'Perhaps I should leave you alone, then.'

'Wait.' The single word was wrenched from him. 'Don't go.'

He felt her surprise as the silence stretched on. She didn't move, either backwards or forwards. He bowed his head.

'I don't want to be alone tonight,' he confessed, his voice low, and then she took a step forward, laid her hand on his shoulder once more.

'You aren't,' she said simply.

Emma didn't know whether it was Larenzo's obvious pain or the attraction that had snapped through the air that had compelled her to stay. Perhaps both. She wanted to comfort him, but she couldn't deny the yearning she had felt uncoil through her body when Larenzo had looked at her with such blatant desire in his eyes. No man had ever looked at her like that before, and it had thrilled her to her core.

The moment stretched on between them as she stood there with her hand still on his shoulder, his head bowed. His skin was warm and smooth underneath her palm, and slowly Larenzo reached up and covered her hand with his own, his fingers twining with hers. The intimacy of the gesture rocked her, sent heat and need and something even deeper and more important spiralling through her. They were simply holding hands, and yet it felt like a pure form of communication, the most intimate thing she'd ever done.

Finally Larenzo broke the moment. He took his hand from hers and turned. Emma could feel the heat rolling off him, inhaled the tangy scent of his aftershave, and desire crashed through her once more. This man was more than a work of art. He was a living, breathing, virile male, and he was close enough for her to touch him. To kiss him. Which she wanted to do, very much.

'Do you have family, Emma?' he asked, startling her out of her haze of desire.

'Y-y-y-yes.'

'Are you close to them?' He gazed at her, his silvery eyes searching her, looking for answers. 'You must not see them very often, living here.'

'I...' How to answer that seemingly innocent question? 'I see my father sometimes. He's currently posted in Budapest, and we've met up occasionally.'

'And your mother?'

Why was he asking her all these questions? She didn't want to talk about her family, and certainly not her mother, yet in the darkened intimacy of the room, of the moment, she knew she would answer. 'No, I'm not close to my mother. My parents divorced when I was twelve, and I didn't see her much after that.'

'That must have been hard.'

A small shrug was all she'd allow on that subject, but Larenzo nodded as if she'd said something important and revealing. 'And siblings? Do you have any sisters or brothers?'

'One sister, Meghan. She lives in New Jersey, does the whole stay-at-home-mom thing.' The kind of life she'd deliberately chosen not to pursue or want. 'We're close. We Skype.' She shook her head in confusion. 'Why are you asking me all this, Larenzo?'

'Because I never had a real family of my own, and I wondered.' He turned, his back to her as he gazed at the fire. 'I wondered how families are. How they're meant to be.'

'What happened to your family?'

'I don't know. My mother left me to fend for myself when I was young, maybe two or three. An orphanage took me in, run by a convent. Not the nicest place. I ran away when I was eleven. Spent the next few years on the street.'

He recited these facts dispassionately, without any self-pity at all, and somehow that made it all the more terrible. 'That's awful. I'm sorry.' Emma would never have guessed such a past for this man, with his wealth and power and magnetism. 'Was this in Palermo?'

'Yes.'

'Those are hard memories.'

'Yes.' He let out a long, low sigh. 'But let's not talk about that tonight.'

'What do you want to talk about?'

'Anything.' He sat down on the sheepskin rug in front of the fire, and patted the floor next to him. Emma came to sit across from him, folding her legs underneath her, conscious of the strangeness of this situation: both of them in their pyjamas, the firelight casting pools of light over their skin, and yet of the ease of it too. It felt weirdly natural to sit there with Larenzo, in the dark, with the fire. Surreal and yet somehow right.

'What do you want to do with your life, Emma?' he asked as he tossed another log on the fire. 'I assume you don't want to be a housekeeper for ever.'

'Would there be something wrong with that?'

He gave a faint, bemused smile. 'No, there's nothing wrong with that. But you are a beautiful, capable young woman, and I imagine you want to see more of the world than a remote Sicilian hilltop.'

'I like to travel,' she admitted. 'I've moved around a lot already.'

'As a diplomat's kid.'

'Yes, and since I finished school. Itchy feet, I suppose.'

'What did you study at school?'

'I did a photography course just for a year, and then I got a backpack and a rail pass and went to see the world.' Determined to enjoy everything life had to offer, never to be tied down, never to be hurt.

'Sounds fun.' He turned to her, an eyebrow arched. 'I think I've seen you with a camera round the place. Have you taken photos here?'

'Yes...'

'May I see them?'

She hesitated, because no one had ever seen her photographs. No one had ever asked. And showing them now to Larenzo felt even more intimate than when they'd held hands. She'd be showing him a part of her soul. 'Okay,' she finally said. 'I'll go get them.' She hurried up to her bedroom, and then leafed through several folders of photos before selecting a few of her favourites. She brought them back to Larenzo, handing them to him silently.

He studied each one carefully, a slight frown puckering his forehead as Emma waited, nibbling her lip. She realised she wanted him to like them, to understand them, and she held her breath as she waited for his verdict.

'They're not holiday snaps,' he said finally and she let out a little laugh.

'No.' She preferred to take candid shots of people, strangers and sometimes friends caught in an unexpected moment, held in thrall by an emotion, whether it was happiness or sorrow or something else.

'This one.' He gestured to a portrait of Rosaria, one of the shopkeepers in Troina. She was sitting on a stool in the back of her bakery, her hands on her thighs, her head thrown back, her face a mass of wrinkles as she let out a deep, belly laugh. 'That's joy,' Larenzo said quietly, and Emma's heart swelled with the knowledge that he did understand, that he'd seen what she'd been trying to capture.

'Yes.'

'I don't think I've ever felt that.' He turned to give her a swift, dark glance. 'Have you?'

Shock rippled through her at the question, and the answer that slipped from her lips without her even realising she was going to say it. 'No,' Emma whispered. 'I don't think I have.' She'd travelled the world, climbed mountains, scuba-dived, done a million and one adventurous and amazing things, had always considered herself a happy person…and yet joy? That kind of deep, abiding, *real* joy?

It had remained beguilingly elusive. And she hadn't realised it until Larenzo had asked her the question.

'You have a skill,' Larenzo said as he turned back to the photographs. 'A true talent. You shouldn't squander it.'

'I'm not—'

'I mean you should exhibit these.' He glanced at her, his eyebrows raised. 'Have you shown them to anyone, to a professional?'

'You're the first person who has seen them.'

He held her gaze, his own darkening. 'Thank you,' he said quietly, and wordlessly Emma nodded.

The moment spun out, stretching and shifting into something else as their gazes remained locked and Emma's breath shortened. A log popped in the fireplace and embers scattered across the hearth, but neither of them so much as twitched.

The desire Emma had felt before now crashed over her in an overpowering wave, obliterating rational thought, obscuring everything but this moment. She wanted this man more than she'd ever wanted anything or anyone before, and as she saw the heat blaze in his eyes she realised with a thrill he felt the same.

Slowly, deliberately, Larenzo reached one hand out towards her, his fingers first skimming her cheek and then his palm cradling her face. The warmth of his palm against her cheek felt electric, every nerve ending she had tingling and quivering with awareness. Larenzo's thumb brushed her mouth, and her lips parted in expectation as a tiny gasp escaped. If he kissed her, she'd be lost. And she knew she wanted to be lost.

His hand tensed briefly against her cheek, and for a terrible second she thought he was going to drop it and move away. This glorious moment would be over. Then he brought his other hand up to frame her face, cradling her between his palms before pulling her inexorably towards him, his lips coming down on hers, soft and hard, cold and hot, everything all at once as a thousand new sensations blazed through her and her mouth opened to his kiss.

Larenzo hauled her towards him, her legs sliding across his as she straddled him, felt the hard press of his arousal against the juncture of her thighs and excitement pulsed hard inside her.

He was kissing her deeply now, with a hungry urgency that Emma felt in herself as she drove her fingers through his hair and pressed even more closely against him, her body arching instinctively as Larenzo pressed back.

After an endless moment that still didn't seem long enough, Larenzo broke off the kiss, his breath coming out in a rush.

'I wasn't going to do that.'

'I wanted you to do it,' she whispered. She couldn't bear it if he stopped now.

He leaned his forehead against hers, their bodies still pressed together, both of their hearts thudding. 'I want you, Emma. I think I want you more than I've ever wanted anyone before.'

A thrill ran through her at this simply stated fact. 'I want you too.'

'But I can't offer you anything other than this night.' He closed his eyes briefly. 'A few hours at most. That's all. That's all it could ever be.'

'I know,' she said softly. When he'd kissed her, she hadn't thought of anything but the moment, yet she acknowledged now that she'd never have expected some kind of commitment from a man like Larenzo. 'I don't want more than this night,' she told him. 'I'm not looking for some kind of relationship, Larenzo, trust me. I just want you, tonight.'

He leaned back a little so he could look into her face. 'If you're sure…?'

She nodded, amazed at just how sure she was. Everything about this night had been surreal, even magical. This felt, bizarrely and yet completely, like the logical and necessary conclusion. 'I'm sure.'

'Then come with me.' He untangled himself from her and rose from the rug in one fluid movement, holding his hand down to help her up. With their fingers linked he led her silently upstairs to his bedroom.

Emma gazed at the king-sized bed with its navy silk sheets she'd changed herself and felt a tremor of—what? Not fear. Anticipation. And a little nervousness, because, while she *was* sure, this was still a new experience. An entirely new experience, and she didn't want to admit to Larenzo just how new it was, how unlike her this decision had been.

He glanced back at her, his fingers still twined with hers. 'Having second thoughts?' he asked quietly, his gaze sweeping over her. 'Cold feet? I wouldn't mind.' He let out a ragged laugh. 'Well, I'd mind, but I'd understand.'

'I'm not having second thoughts.' She swallowed, lifted her chin. She wouldn't tell him about her inexperience. It didn't matter to her, and she didn't want it to matter to him, or put him off. 'Are you?' she challenged, and he let out a soft huff of laughter.

'Definitely not.' He tugged her towards him. 'Come here, Emma.'

And she came willingly, her breasts pressing against his bare chest as his mouth came down on hers once more and for a few blissful, buzzing seconds she forgot everything but the hunger and need for this, for him.

Larenzo reached down and with one swift tug he had her T-shirt up and over her head; the feel of her breasts brushing the crisp hair on his chest was so intense it almost hurt. She'd never felt so much, felt so alive, not when she'd been on top of a mountain or deep in the ocean. All her adventures paled in light of this.

She let out a gasp that he muffled with his mouth, his hands sliding down her back and then cupping her bottom as he settled her against his arousal.

He moved his mouth from her lips to the curve of her neck, the touch of his tongue against her sensitive skin making her shiver.

Then he drew her to the bed, laying her down on top of the silken sheets and covering her body with his own.

She twined her arms around his neck and arched up towards him, craving the connection of their bodies fused in every place. Of being that close to another person... even if it was just for a single night. A few hours. And she knew Larenzo needed it too, craved it as much as she did. She was giving him herself, the only comfort she could offer him now.

Larenzo slid a hand between her thighs, slipping her pyjama shorts down her legs and then tossing them on the floor. The feel of his fingers against her most sensitive flesh had Emma arching upwards again, her head thrown back as sensations fizzed and popped inside her.

And then they exploded and her breath rushed out on a ragged cry as Larenzo worked magic with his fingers and left her boneless in his arms.

'Oh...'

'That's just to start,' he promised with a soft laugh, and then he tossed his own pyjama bottoms aside before he slid seamlessly inside her—and then stopped. 'Emma...'

She saw the confusion on his face, the uncertainty, and knew he'd guessed her inexperience. 'You haven't...' he began slowly and she answered by tilting her hips up.

'It doesn't matter,' she said fiercely, and as her body found its instinctive rhythm Larenzo matched it, burying his head in the curve of her shoulder as his body surged into hers.

If she'd felt any pain or discomfort, it was long gone as the exquisite friction of Larenzo's body created a pleasure deeper and fiercer than what she'd already felt at his experienced hands.

She let out another long, ragged cry as the sensations exploded inside her again and with a shudder Larenzo emptied himself into her and then was still.

They lay like that for a few seconds before he wrapped his arms around her and rolled onto his back.

'Why didn't you tell me you were a virgin?' he asked quietly.

Emma could still feel him inside her, still feel the bone-melting ripples of pleasure that had utterly rocked her moments before. 'Because like I said, it didn't matter.'

'I might have done things differently...'

'I liked the way you did things.'

He laughed softly then, his arms tightening around her. 'Thank you, Emma,' he said quietly, and she wasn't quite sure what he was thanking her for. She propped herself on her elbows to gaze down at him, and saw the ravages of both grief and pleasure on his face. She had no regrets, and yet she still wished she could smooth the furrows of worry from his forehead. She brushed his hair from his eyes instead, savouring the feel of him.

'I should be thanking you,' she said, and Larenzo smiled faintly before glancing out at the night sky; the moon was on the wane, dawn only an hour or two away. 'You should sleep.'

Did he want her to leave? Uncertainly Emma started to roll off him, but Larenzo clasped her to him once more.

'Stay,' he said, his voice rough with emotion. 'Stay until morning.'

And so she did.

CHAPTER THREE

THEY CAME AT DAWN. Larenzo heard the first car drive up, the crunch of gravel, the sound of a car door shutting quietly, as if they were trying to hide their presence. As if they could.

He stilled, every muscle tensing, Emma still in his arms. *Emma.* He would spare her an ugly scene. She deserved so much more than that, but that was all he could give her now.

Slowly he slipped from the bed, doing his best not to disturb her. She sighed in her sleep and turned, her tousled hair falling across one cheek, a tendril lying across her breast.

He gazed at her for a moment, drinking her in: the golden, freckled skin, the wavy golden-brown hair, her lashes fanned out on her cheeks, although he knew if she opened her eyes, they would be golden-green. His golden girl for a night, gone in the morning.

At least he would be gone.

Quickly Larenzo turned, reaching for his jeans. He pulled on a rugby shirt and ran his hands through his hair, took a deep breath. And looked one last time at Emma, at freedom and happiness, pleasure and peace. He'd known them all with her last night, and now they were nothing but memories. Resolutely he turned from her and left the room.

Emma awoke to the thud of boots on the stairs, the sound of stomping down the hall. She was still blinking the sleep from her eyes, one hand reaching for the sheet to cover herself, her mind barely processing what she'd heard, when the door was thrown open and three men crowded there, all of them glaring at her. Her heart seemed to still in her chest, everything in her going numb with horror as she stared at these strange men.

'What—?'

They spoke in rapid Italian, too fast for her to understand, although during her two years in Sicily she'd become fairly conversant in the language. Still, she understood their tone. Their derision and contempt.

She clutched the sheet to her breasts, her whole body trembling with indignation and fear. *'Chi sei? Cosa stai facendo?'* Who are you, and what are you doing? They didn't answer.

One man, clearly the leader of the pack, ripped the sheet away from her naked body. Emma gasped in shock. *'Puttana.'* He spat the single word. Whore.

Emma shook her head, her mouth dry, her body still trembling. She felt as if she'd awakened to an alternate reality, a horrible nightmare, and she had no idea how to make it stop. *Where was Larenzo?*

One of the men grabbed her by the arm and yanked her upwards. She came, stumbling, trying futilely to cover herself. He reached for her T-shirt and shorts discarded on the floor and threw them at her.

'You are English?' he asked, his voice clipped, and she nodded.

'American. And my consulate will hear—'

He cut her off with a hard laugh. 'Get dressed. You're coming with us.'

Quickly, clumsily, Emma yanked on her clothes. Dressed, even if only in flimsy pyjamas, she felt a little braver. 'Where is Signor Cavelli?' she asked in Italian.

The man eyed her scornfully. 'Downstairs, at the moment. But he'll spend the rest of his life in prison.'

Emma's mouth dropped open. *Prison?* What on earth was he talking about? Were these awful men police?

'Come on,' the man commanded her tersely, and with her mind spinning she followed the men downstairs.

Larenzo stood in the centre of the sitting room, his eyes blazing silver fire as he caught sight of her.

'You are all right? They didn't hurt you?'

'Shut up!' The words were like the crack of a gunshot as one of the men slapped Larenzo across the face. He didn't even blink, although Emma could see the red imprint of the man's hand on Larenzo's cheek.

'They didn't hurt me,' she said quietly and the man turned on her.

'Enough. Neither of you are to speak to one another. Who knows what you might try to communicate?'

'She has nothing to do with any of it,' Larenzo said, and he sounded scornful, as if he were actually in control of the situation. With an icy ripple of shock Emma saw that he was handcuffed. 'Do you actually think I'd tell a woman, my housekeeper no less, anything of value?'

The words, spoken so derisively, shouldn't have hurt. She knew, intellectually at least, that he was trying to protect her, although from what she had no idea. Even so they did hurt, just as the look Larenzo gave her, a look as derisive as those of the *carabinieri*, did.

'She's nothing to me.'

'Even so, she'll be taken in for questioning,' the man replied shortly and Larenzo's eyes blazed once more.

'She knows nothing. She's American. Do you want the consulate all over this?'

'*This*,' the man snapped, poking a finger into Larenzo's chest, 'is the biggest sting we've had in Sicily for twenty years. I don't give a damn about the consulate.'

They'd been speaking Italian, and, while Emma had caught the gist of it, she still didn't understand what was going on.

'Please, let me get dressed properly,' she said, her voice coming out croaky as she stumbled over the Italian. 'And then I'll go with you and answer any questions you might have.'

The man turned to glare at her with narrowed eyes. Then he gave a brief nod, and, with another policeman accompanying her, Emma went upstairs to her bedroom. The man waited outside the room while she pulled on underwear, jeans, a long-sleeved T-shirt, and a fleece. She brushed her teeth and hair, grabbed her purse and her passport, and then, just in case, she took her backpack and put a change of clothes, her camera, and her folder of photographs in it. Who knew when she'd be able to return? Just the realisation sent another icy wave of terror crashing through her.

Taking a deep, steadying breath, she left the room. The man accompanied her downstairs; the front door was open and she saw several cars outside. Larenzo was being shoved into one. She turned to the man.

'Where are we going?'

'Palermo.'

'Palermo? But that's nearly three hours away—'

The man smiled coldly. 'So it is. I'm afraid you'll have to be so inconvenienced.'

Three hours later Emma sat in an interrogation room at the anti-Mafia headquarters of Palermo's police department. She'd been given a paper cup of cold coffee and made to wait until finally the man who had made the arrest back at Larenzo's villa came and sat down across from her, putting his elbows on the chipped tabletop.

'You know your boyfriend is in a lot of trouble.'

Emma closed her eyes briefly. She was aching with exhaustion, numb with confusion and fear, and she missed Larenzo desperately even as she forced herself to remember she hadn't actually known him all that well. *Until last night. Until he held me in his arms and made me feel cherished and important.* 'He's not my boyfriend.'

'Whoever he is. He's going to prison, probably for the rest of his life.'

Emma licked her dry lips. 'What…what has he done?'

'You don't know?'

'I have no idea. All I know is he was—is—CEO of Cavelli Enterprises.' And that when he kissed her her mind emptied of thoughts. He made her body both buzz and sing. But then words began to ricochet through her, words Larenzo had spoken to her last night. *It's my own fault.* What had he done?

The man must have seen something of this in her face for he leaned forward. 'You know something.'

'No.'

'I've been doing this for a long time.' He sounded almost kind. 'I can tell, *signorina.* I can tell when someone is lying.'

'I'm not lying. I don't know anything. I don't even know what Cavelli Enterprises did.'

'And if I told you Larenzo Cavelli was involved with the Mafia? You wouldn't know anything about that?'

Bile rose in her throat and she swallowed hard. 'No, I certainly wouldn't.'

'It didn't concern you, the amount of security he had for that villa?'

She thought of his insistence on locking the doors, the elaborate security system. 'No.'

'Don't play dumb with me, *signorina.*'

'Look, maybe I was dumb, but I really didn't know.' Emma's voice rose in agitation. 'Plenty of people have detailed security systems.'

'Cavelli never said anything to you?'

Again his words raced through her mind. The grief on his face, the resignation she'd heard in his voice, the sense that everything was over, that this was his last night. He must have known they were coming to arrest him. He must have realised his activities had been discovered. Even so she couldn't reconcile the man she'd known, however briefly, with the Mafia. And yet as tender a lover as Larenzo had been, he was still virtually a stranger. She had no idea what he'd got up to when he'd been away from the villa. No idea at all.

'*Signorina?*'

'Please,' Emma said wearily. 'I was his housekeeper. I barely saw him. I don't know anything.'

Eight endless hours later she was finally released from the police. When she asked about returning to the villa, the man at the desk shook his head.

'The villa is being searched by the police. Everything there is potential evidence. You won't be able to go back for some time.'

And so Emma headed out into the busy streets of Palermo, mopeds and sports cars speeding by, her mind spinning as she tried to think what to do now. She had no real reason to go all the way back to the villa. She had nothing of value there but a few clothes and photography books.

But where could she go?

She ended up at a cheap hotel near the train station; she sat on the single bed, her backpack at her feet, her whole life in tatters.

She told herself she was used to moving on, and it would be easy enough to look for a new job. She could spend some time with her father in Budapest while she decided where she wanted to go, what she wanted to do.

And yet that prospect seemed bleak rather than hopeful; she might be used to moving on, but she hadn't been ready this time. She'd liked her life in Sicily. The villa had been the closest thing she'd ever known to a home.

And as for Larenzo…

She'd known, of course she'd known, that their one night together wasn't going anywhere. But it had still *meant* something. She'd felt a deep connection to him last night, an understanding and a tenderness… Had it all been false? According to the police, he was a Mafioso. The inspector had told her they had incontrovertible evidence, had said there were photos, witnesses, files. Everything to convict Larenzo Cavelli of too many horrible crimes. Extortion, the police had said. Theft. Assault. Organised delinquency, which was the legal term for involvement in the Mafia.

Faced with all of it, Emma knew she had no choice but to believe. Larenzo Cavelli was a criminal.

The next morning, after a sleepless night, Emma went to an Internet café to arrange her passage to Budapest. Yet as she clicked on a website for cheap airfares, she realised she didn't want to go there. She didn't want to traipse around Europe, taking odd jobs, at least not yet. She wanted to go somewhere safe, somewhere far away from all this, to recover and heal. She wanted to see her sister. Quickly Emma took out her mobile and scrolled through for Meghan's number.

'Emma?' Concern sharpened her sister's voice as she answered the call. 'You sound…'

'I'm tired. And a bit overwhelmed.' She didn't want to go into the details of what had happened on the phone; they were too recent, too raw, and she was afraid she might burst into tears right in the middle of the Internet café. 'My job in Sicily has ended suddenly, and I thought I'd come for a visit, if you don't mind having me.'

'Of course I don't mind having you,' Meghan exclaimed. 'Ryan will be delighted to see you.'

Emma pictured her tousle-haired three-year-old nephew with a tired smile. It had been too long since she'd seen him or her sister. 'Great. I'm going to book a flight for tomorrow if I can.'

'Let me know the time and we'll pick you up from the airport.'

Twenty-four hours later Emma touched down in New York and, after clearing immigration, she walked straight into her sister's arms.

'Is everything okay?' Meghan asked as she hugged her tightly. Emma nodded wordlessly. Nothing felt right at that moment, but she hoped it would soon. All she needed was a little time to get over this, and then she'd be back on the road, taking photographs, looking for adventure, as footloose as ever. The prospect didn't fill her with anything except a weary desolation.

She spent the next week mainly sleeping and spending time with Ryan and Meghan; she wanted to shut the world out, but she couldn't quite do it, and especially not when her sister looked up from *The New York Times* one morning, her eyes narrowed.

'I'm just reading an article about how business CEO Larenzo Cavelli was arrested for being involved in the Mafia.' Emma felt the colour drain from her face but said nothing. 'Wasn't that your boss, Emma?'

'Yes.'

'That's why your job ended?'

Emma nodded jerkily as she poured some orange juice. 'Yes.'

'You were working for someone in the *Mafia*?'

'I didn't know, Meghan!'

Meghan sat back in her chair, her eyes wide. 'Of course you didn't know. But good gracious, Emma. I'm so glad you're here, and you're safe.'

Emma closed her eyes briefly. She could picture Larenzo as he braced himself above her, his face suffused with tenderness as he gave her more pleasure than she'd ever known or thought possible. And then just hours later, when she'd heard the thud of the boots in the hall, the men glaring at her as they ripped the sheet away from her body...

'So am I,' she said quietly. 'So am I.'

After that she couldn't shut out the world any more. She read in the newspaper that Larenzo had confessed to everything, and there would be no trial. Within a month of her arrival he'd been sentenced to life in prison.

Two days after that, Emma realised she hadn't got her period that month. One three-minute test later, she discovered the truth. She was pregnant with Larenzo Cavelli's child.

CHAPTER FOUR

Eighteen months later

'Look at me, Aunt Emma!'

Emma waved to her nephew as he clambered to the top of the climbing frame at the playground near her sister's house. It was late October, and the leaves of the maple trees in the little park were scarlet, the sky above a cloudless blue. It was a beautiful, crisp day, and yet even so she couldn't keep herself from picturing the mountains of Sicily, and remembering how clear and pure the air was up there at this time of year.

Shivering slightly in the chill wind, Emma told herself to stop thinking about Sicily. She would never go back there. Never see the Nebrodi mountains again. *Never see Larenzo Cavelli again.*

Which was just as well, considering the man was a criminal.

Instinctively her gaze moved to the stroller a few feet away, where her daughter Ava was sleeping peacefully. She was ten months old, born on Christmas Eve, and Emma still marvelled at her. Still marvelled at the way her own life had changed so drastically.

When she'd discovered she was pregnant, she'd been shocked and numb for days, as well as embarrassed that she hadn't even *thought* about birth control when she'd been with Larenzo. That was how much he'd affected her. How much she'd wanted him in that moment.

Meghan, as eagle-eyed as ever, had guessed she was pregnant within a matter of days, and Emma had ended up telling her sister everything.

'What do you want to do?' Meghan had asked in her direct way as they'd sat at her kitchen table, Emma shredding tissues while Meghan got up to make tea. 'I love babies,' she continued as she switched on the kettle, 'and I think each one is a blessing, but I'll support you no matter what.'

'Thank you,' Emma had answered, sniffing. 'Truthfully, I don't know what to do. I never planned on marrying or having a family...not that marriage is a possibility in this case.'

'Why haven't you?' Meghan asked, one hip braced against the counter as she fixed Emma with a thoughtful stare. 'Most people think about being with someone, at least.'

'I don't know.' Emma shredded another tissue, avoiding her sister's perceptive gaze. 'You know me. I like to be on the move. See new things. I don't want to be held down.'

'And a baby is the ultimate in being held down,' Meghan answered with a sigh.

'Yes...' Which made it seem simple, but Emma felt as if nothing was.

'I know Mom leaving affected you badly, Em,' Meghan said quietly. 'More than it did me. I was at college. I was already out of the way.'

'She was your mother too,' Emma answered, still not looking at her sister. By silent agreement she and Meghan had never really talked about their mother. Emma hadn't even seen her in at least five years. Louise Leighton had moved to Arizona with her second husband when Emma was still in high school; Emma had spent a wretched few months out in Arizona with her, but it had been awkward and stilted and just generally awful, and she'd left pretty quickly, after one blazing argument. Her mother hadn't protested.

Since then, beyond a few pithy emails, her mother had never made any attempt to contact her. She didn't know if Meghan was in touch with her or not; she'd never asked, told herself she didn't care.

'Anyway,' Meghan resumed, 'what I'm trying to say is, I understand if motherhood scares you. You didn't have the best example.'

'I'm not scared,' Emma answered. She pressed a hand against her middle, almost as if she could feel the tiny life moving inside her. 'I just feel like my whole life has been upended. Everything that happened in Sicily…' She trailed off, fighting against the memories that continued to swamp her, and Meghan came over to give her a hug.

'It's hard,' she said. 'And you have some time.'

As the days slipped by Emma had come to accept this new life inside her, and realise that, to her amazement, she actually welcomed it. She watched her sister with Ryan and knew she wanted that same kind of bond, that closeness with another person. Already she felt a surprising and unshakeable love for this person who was a part of her.

Once she had pictured her life unspooling like a rainbow-coloured thread as she traipsed about the world, having adventure after adventure. But perhaps motherhood would be the greatest adventure of all.

It had been that, she thought now as she gazed at her sleeping daughter. From the moment she'd been born, dark-haired and grey-eyed, Ava had possessed the Cavelli charisma. Whether she was screaming to be fed or simply demanding to be heard, the force of her personality could not be denied. She was her father's daughter.

And her father was serving life in prison.

Emma had had a year and a half to become accustomed to the fact that Larenzo was a Mafioso, and yet the knowledge still had the power to stun her. She couldn't look back on their one night together without experiencing a shaft of bittersweet longing, as well as a sense of bewilderment that the man she'd thought she'd known, at least a little, was someone else entirely.

'Are you almost ready to go?' Meghan asked as she walked up to her in the park. Her cheeks were red with cold and she cradled a thermos of coffee. 'Ryan will want his lunch before playgroup, and, if I'm not mistaken, your little madam is going to wake up soon and want hers.'

'Undoubtedly.' With a wry look for her sleeping daughter, Emma reached for the handles of the pram.

'Emma…' Meghan began, and Emma tensed instinctively. She'd known a conversation was coming; she'd been living with Meghan and her husband, Pete, for over eighteen months now. They'd been happy to support her through her pregnancy and she'd taken a few odd cleaning jobs until she'd been too ungainly to manage it, in order to contribute to the household expenses.

Then Ava had been born, and her life had become a sleepless whirlwind; she'd stood in its centre, dazed and helpless to do much other than care for this baby that still managed to startle her with her existence.

But her daughter would be a year soon and Emma knew she needed to find her own way. Make her own life, for her own sake as well as her sister's.

'I know,' she said quietly, her gaze on Ava sleeping in the pram, the pink blanket pulled up to her chin, which had a cleft the same as Larenzo's. 'I need to get a move on.'

'No.' Meghan put a hand on Emma's arm. 'I wasn't going to say that. I'd never say that, Emma. You're welcome to stay with us as long as you like. Always.'

Emma shook her head. She knew her sister meant well,

but she also knew that she couldn't stay. She hadn't contributed anything to the household finances since Ava's birth, and she and Ava had taken up the spare bedroom for far too long. Meghan and Pete wanted more children, and they needed the space.

'I've been meaning to get my act together for months now,' she told her sister. 'I've just—' she let out a long, low breath '—felt frozen, I suppose. And keeping Ava fed and changed has taken more energy than I care to admit.' She let out a shaky laugh. 'I don't know how you do it.'

'Motherhood is never easy, and Ava is a demanding baby,' Meghan answered. 'But this isn't about me or Pete, Emma. It's about you. What's best for you. I want you to have your own life. Maybe meet someone...'

Emma shook her head. She couldn't even *think* about meeting someone. She might not have loved Larenzo Cavelli or had her heart broken, but even so something in her felt a little dented. A bit bruised. And she'd never been interested in a serious relationship anyway. She was even less so now, with a bad experience and a baby in tow.

'I know I need to get a job.'

'It's not about money—'

'But it is, Meghan, at least in part. As wonderful as you are, you can't support me for ever. I'm twenty-seven years old, and I chose to have a child. I need to step up.' She took a deep breath. 'I know I seem like a sleep-deprived zombie most of the time, but I have been thinking about possibilities. Maybe moving to New York and getting a job there, something to do with photography.'

As far as a plan went, it wasn't very sensible, and Emma could tell her sister thought so from the look on her face. 'New York? But it's so expensive. And I'm not sure there are too many jobs in photography going...'

'I know, but...' The other option was staying in New Jersey, finding some poky apartment she could afford on the salary she'd get as a waitress or cleaner, the only kind of job for which she was qualified. 'I like to dream,' she admitted with a wry sigh, and Meghan nodded in understanding.

'What about another job as a housekeeper? A live-in position, so you could have Ava with you?'

'I'm not sure there are many of those going around.'

'You only need one.'

'True.' Emma glanced down at her daughter, who was starting to stir, her little face turning red as she screwed her features up in preparation for one of her ear-splitting howls. 'We'd better get going,' she told Meghan. 'Princess Ava needs her lunch.'

Back at the house she and Meghan fed Ava and Ryan, and then ate their own lunch while the two children played nearby.

'All right, let's do this,' Meghan said, ever practical, and resolutely Emma nodded as her sister pulled her laptop towards her and brought up the webpage for an agency that supplied jobs in the cleaning and hospitality industries.

Emma suppressed a groan as some of the available jobs scrolled by: night-time cleaning at a business park in Newark, janitorial work in a local elementary school.

'I don't…' she began, but Meghan cut her off with a quick shake of her head.

'We'll find something. Something perfect. There's no rush.'

But there *was* a rush, Emma thought glumly, even if she didn't want to say as much to her sister. Meghan might be happy to have her stay indefinitely, but she wasn't always so sure about Pete; as the breadwinner he surely felt the strain on the family finances more than anyone.

And she also knew she wanted more for her life than living in a spare bedroom, changing diapers and dreaming of sleep.

Maybe a poky apartment and a job cleaning school toilets would be it, at least for the interim. If she was careful she could save enough money to go somewhere, maybe travel again, this time with Ava. She pictured herself working her way through Europe, her baby in a backpack, and, while it held a certain quirky charm, she was also realistic enough to acknowledge how difficult that would be.

She could, she supposed, go to stay with her father, but he had been decidedly nonplussed about his unmarried daughter having a baby by a man who was serving a life sentence in prison, and in any case her father was immersed in his work, as he had been since his wife had left him fifteen years ago. He hadn't even seen Ava yet.

No, she needed to do something on her own. Stand on her own two feet, however wobbly she was.

'Let me have a look,' she said, and pulled the laptop towards her. She browsed the jobs for a few more minutes, taking down details, until Ava started crying, ready for her afternoon nap.

'I'll take her upstairs,' Emma said, scooping her protesting daughter into her arms. Ava wrapped her chubby arms around Emma's neck and snuffled against her chest. Her daughter was demanding, even difficult, but she still managed to make Emma's heart melt with love. She'd never regret her decision, even if she ended up cleaning toilets for the rest of her life.

Life could still be an adventure, she told herself as she settled Ava in her crib. It was all about attitude. No matter where she was or what she did, she could still enjoy her daughter, maybe even try photography again. She hadn't picked up her camera since Ava's birth, except to take a few photos of her daughter. The spontaneous, candid moments she'd captured on film all over the world had been hard to find here, and Emma had been too exhausted and overwhelmed to look for them.

She was just coming downstairs, Ava asleep hopefully for at least an hour and Meghan at playgroup with Ryan, when the doorbell sounded. Hoping the noise wouldn't wake Ava, ever a light sleeper, Emma went to answer it.

And stared straight into the face of Larenzo Cavelli. Shock blazed through her as she looked at him; he was thinner, the angles of his cheekbones a little sharper, everything about him a bit harder. A faint scar ran down one cheek, starting by his eyebrow and ending at his jaw. She noticed these changes distantly, her mind dazed and spinning; she could not actually believe it was him. He was here. How? And *why*?

'Larenzo...' she finally managed, her voice a rasp, and his face didn't show so much as a flicker of emotion as he answered.

'Hello, Emma.'

Larenzo gazed at Emma dispassionately; she was clearly shocked to see him, but he felt nothing when he looked at her, except perhaps a twinge of remorse, a flicker of bittersweet memory. That night they'd shared so long ago felt as if it had happened to someone else. It *had* happened to someone else. Eighteen months in prison changed you. For ever.

'May I come in?' He took a step towards her and she drew her breath in sharply, one hand fluttering to her throat.

'Don't—' she began, and he stilled. She almost looked afraid. Afraid of him.

'Do you think I'm going to hurt you?' he asked, wondering why he was surprised. Everyone else had believed the worst of him. Why shouldn't she?

Emma's eyes widened, her hand still at her throat. 'I don't—I don't know. Why are you here, Larenzo?'

Her voice wavered; she really was afraid. She thought

he was *dangerous*. It should have occurred to him before, of course. He'd thought all of his naive delusions about humanity had been stripped away, but clearly he'd clung to this last one. The memory of his one night with Emma had sustained him through prison. He didn't like having it tarnished now.

'I'm here,' he finally said, his voice cool, 'because I felt I owed you something.'

'You don't.'

'Considering your employment with me ended so abruptly, I thought you deserved some recompense,' he continued as if she hadn't spoken.

'Recompense...'

He stepped past her and dropped the envelope with the bank draft onto the hall table. 'Six months' pay. I thought you should have it.'

She stared at the envelope with something like revulsion. 'I don't want your money,' she said in a low voice. 'I don't want anything from you.'

'This money was honestly earned,' Larenzo informed her coldly. 'I can promise you that.'

'Why should I believe anything you say?' she shot back. 'How are you even *here*? The judge gave you life in prison—'

'I was released last week. Clearly you don't read the papers.'

'No, I...' She licked her lips, her gaze still wide. 'I haven't had time.'

'Well, if you'd read them,' Larenzo said, his voice coming out in a cold drawl, 'you would have known that all the charges against me were dropped.'

'They were?' She looked bewildered, her gaze darting between him and the stairs. Was she thinking of making a run for it, barricading herself in a bedroom? Did she really think he was going to *hurt* her? He was caught between fury and despair at the thought, and then he blanked out both emotions. He might have held onto the memory of Emma through prison, and their night together might have compelled him to find her now, but he didn't actually feel anything for her. He couldn't feel anything at all.

'Yes, they were. Otherwise I wouldn't be here. Obviously. Unless you thought I'd escaped?' He arched an eyebrow, smiled as if this were all so very amusing. 'Stage-managed some sort of breakout?'

'I...I don't know what I think.' She walked slowly past him, to the small sitting room at the front of the house. Larenzo followed her, watched as she sank onto the sofa, her head in her hands.

'How did you find me here?' she asked after a long, silent moment, her head still bowed.

'This was the address you gave on your employment application.'

She glanced up at him, her eyes widening once more. 'And you came all the way to America to give me six months' pay? If you really possessed such a conscience to see me adequately *recompensed*, you could have just deposited it in my bank account. You should have my details from when I was in your employment.'

Larenzo's mouth tightened. 'I was in America anyway.' She shook her head slowly, still dazed. Larenzo let his gaze rove over her, remembering her golden skin, her laughing eyes that looked so serious and dark now. She looked different, he realised. More womanly. She must have gained a little weight, and yet it suited her. Her breasts were fuller under the soft pink sweater she wore, and her face was a bit rounder. Her skin was as golden as he'd remembered, her golden-brown hair wavy and tousled about her face. His golden girl. What a joke.

'Why are you in America?' she asked and Larenzo snapped his gaze away from her.

'I'm relocating to New York.'

'New York—'

'Is that a problem?' he enquired coolly. 'I only came here to give you your pay.'

'I know, but…' She glanced up towards the stairs once more, and Larenzo's gaze narrowed. That was the second time she'd done that. What was upstairs? Was Emma hiding something from him? God knew he'd learned to become suspicious of everyone and everything. Trust was a concept he no longer even remotely considered.

'It doesn't matter,' she said quickly, as if coming to a decision. She rose from the sofa. 'Thank you for the six months' pay. That was…kind of you, considering.'

'Considering?' he repeated, his gaze narrowing. 'Considering what?'

Colour washed Emma's cheeks. 'Just the situation…'

'You mean considering I'm a criminal? Is that what you mean, Emma?' He didn't know why he was pushing her, only that he was. That he wanted her to say it, admit what she thought of him. Perhaps it would be like lancing a wound.

Emma lifted her chin, her eyes flashing in challenge. 'And what if it was?'

'I thought you knew me better than that.'

'I didn't know you at all, Larenzo. You were my employer, and I saw you a few times. We never even had a proper conversation before—' She stopped abruptly, the colour deepening in her cheeks as she looked away.

'Before what?' he demanded, his voice low and insistent. He was punishing himself as much as her by raking this all up, bringing the memories he'd tormented himself with to the fore. 'Before I made love to you? Before you wrapped your legs around my waist and—'

'Don't.' The single word came out in a suffocated whisper. 'Don't remind me.'

Larenzo's lip curled. 'You don't want to remember?'

'Of course I don't.' She glared at him, her golden-green eyes full of misery. 'I don't know why you were released from prison, Larenzo, or why the charges against you were dropped, but I just want you out of my life.' She pressed her lips together as she held his stare. 'I trust that won't be an issue.'

'An issue?' he repeated. Fury beat through his veins, fired his blood. 'I came here as a matter of courtesy. Clearly the effort was wasted.'

'I think it's best if you go now.'

'Fine.' He nodded curtly and curled his hands into fists at his sides, not trusting himself not to grab her by the shoulders and demand to know what he'd ever done to make her think he was a mobster. A Mafioso. *Mio Dio*, how could everyone he'd ever known have judged him so harshly and completely?

Because the evidence had been there, thanks to Bertrano. Because he'd confessed, even if he'd felt he had no choice.

She held his gaze, her chin still lifted, her shoulders thrown back, standing proud and defiant even though he knew she was afraid. Of him.

He opened his mouth to say something of his innocence, but then he closed it. Why claim something she would never believe? 'Goodbye,' he said instead, and turned towards the hallway.

A child's cry suddenly echoed from upstairs. From the corner of his eye he saw Emma freeze, her face drain of colour. He wouldn't have thought anything of the cry, considering he knew Emma was living with her sister and her family. And yet...

The child cried again, the plaintive wail of a baby. Emma didn't move. Neither did Larenzo. Every sense he had was on alert, although for what he could not say.

'Aren't you going to go to the child?' he asked, his voice deliberately mild as the baby continued to cry, the sobs becoming louder and more urgent.

Emma swallowed, and he watched the workings of her slender throat. 'I will. When you leave.'

He gazed at her for a taut moment, saw how her eyes had become huge golden pools in a face drained of colour. 'Is it your sister's child? Why is she not going to fetch the *bambino*?'

'She's not here.' Emma licked her lips, and Larenzo thought he saw panic in that wide gaze. 'Please, Larenzo. Just go.'

'I will.' He cocked his head towards the stairs. 'But maybe you should get the *bambino* first.'

'No.' The word came out like a gunshot, fast and loud. Larenzo raised his eyebrows. Emma stared him down. 'I told you, I don't want you here. Now go.' Her voice rose in a raggedy edge of terror, and Larenzo took a step towards her.

'What are you hiding from me, Emma?'

'Nothing—' But it sounded feeble. He took another step towards her.

'Tell me the truth. You're hiding something. I don't know what it could be, but—'

'What do you think I'm hiding from you?' she cut him off scornfully. She nodded towards the stairs. 'A *baby*?'

The words hung there, seeming to echo through the sudden silence of the room. Larenzo stared at her, saw how bloodless her lips were as they parted soundlessly.

The thought hadn't fully formed in his mind until she'd said the words. He'd sensed she was hiding something, had felt her panic and fear, had heard the baby cry...

And yet it hadn't all come together for him. But it did now, crystallising with shocking clarity, and without a word for her he turned from the room and bounded up the stairs.

'Larenzo—' She hurried after him, one arm flung towards him in desperate supplication. 'Larenzo, please, don't—'

He could hear the child crying, the voice pitiful and plaintive. 'Mama. Mama.'

'Please,' she said again, choking on the word, and Larenzo ignored her.

Mama. Mama.

He threw open the door and came to a complete and stunned halt as he saw the baby standing in her crib, chubby fists gripping the rail, cherubic face screwed up and wet with tears.

Emma came into the room behind him, breathing hard, and the baby flung her arms out towards her. 'Mama.'

And Larenzo knew. He would have known just by looking at the child, with her ink-dark hair and large grey eyes, the cleft in her chin. He turned to Emma, who was gazing at him with undisguised panic.

'When,' he asked in a low, deadly voice, 'were you going to tell me about my child?'

CHAPTER FIVE

EMMA STARED AT Larenzo and saw the fury blazing in his gaze. Why, oh, why had she said that about hiding a baby? She'd meant to be bold, to pour scorn on the presumption, but she'd seen how she'd given him the idea instead. She'd told him about Ava.

Now she sagged against the doorway, completely at a loss as to what to do or say. Larenzo took a step towards her, his hands balled into fists.

'So this is why you were so desperate for me to leave—'

'Mama,' Ava called, her arms still outstretched, and Emma straightened and walked swiftly towards her daughter, scooping her up in her arms, and pressed her cheek against Ava's downy hair.

'Please,' she murmured to Larenzo. 'Let me settle her and then we'll talk.' Although what she could tell him, she had no idea. She'd never imagined this happening, ever. She'd never expected even to see Larenzo again.

Ava continued to snuffle against her chest and Emma soothed her mindlessly, her mind spinning in futile circles. She settled her back in the cot as Larenzo waited in the hall and hoped her daughter might drift off to sleep once more. She'd slept for only twenty minutes, which unfortunately wasn't that uncommon, but on a good day Emma could count on an hour.

Quietly she slipped out of the room and closed the door. Larenzo stood there, arms folded, eyebrows raised. He opened his mouth to speak but Emma shook her head and pressed a finger to her lips, cocking her head to indicate he should follow her downstairs.

In the kitchen she wiped the counters and tidied up the last of the lunch dishes, needing to keep busy, to keep from thinking how on earth she was going to handle this. Handle *him*. Larenzo watched her, one powerful shoulder propped against the doorway, everything about him arrogant, assured and definitely intimidating. She couldn't *handle* this man at all.

'You do not deny she's mine,' he said finally, and Emma shook her head.

'How can I? She looks just like you.'

'Yes.' He raked a hand through his hair, his gaze shuttered and distant as he shook his head slowly. 'We didn't use birth control.'

'No.'

'I never even thought...'

'Nor did I. Obviously.'

'She must have put a dent in your plans,' he said after a moment, his voice turning sharp, and Emma narrowed her eyes.

'What do you mean?'

'All your travel plans. You told me you liked to move around. Itchy feet, you said.'

She was surprised and weirdly gratified that he'd remembered what she'd said, but also piqued that he was throwing it back in her face now. 'That changed when I became pregnant.'

'You never considered a termination?'

Her mouth dropped open. 'Is that what you would have preferred? Because—'

'No.' He shook his head, one swift, violent movement. '*No.* But I could understand if—'

She let out a rush of breath. 'I thought of it at first, I

suppose, but never seriously. I never thought I wanted a husband or children, but I couldn't…she was a part of me.' A lump formed in her throat and resolutely she swallowed past it. 'I loved her even before she was born.'

'And you've been living here since her birth?' His gaze moved around the small kitchen, and Emma prickled.

'My sister has been very kind—'

'Yes, of course. But what about your father? Is he still in Budapest?'

So he remembered that too. 'Yes, he is, but I wanted to be here. And frankly he wasn't thrilled about me being pregnant, unmarried, and the father—'

'In prison,' he finished flatly, and Emma nodded.

'In any case, we're fine here.'

'But you can't stay here for ever.'

'Meghan is happy for us to stay,' Emma shot back. She wasn't about to admit to Larenzo that she might need to move out. 'Anyway, I don't see how this concerns you, Larenzo—'

'Are you serious?' He cut her off, his voice harsh. 'She's my daughter.' He paused, struggling to control his emotions while Emma watched in apprehension. 'What's her name?' he finally asked.

She hesitated, reluctant to part with even that much information. What if Larenzo wanted to be a part of Ava's life, of their lives? How on earth could she cope with that?

'Emma, I deserve to know her name!' His voice came out raggedly, and with a shaft of guilt Emma remembered how he'd told her about his childhood in Palermo, how he'd never had a real family. And with that came other memories of their night together, tender ones that she'd tried to keep herself from remembering. They tumbled through her mind in a bittersweet rush of poignant longing and she was helpless against it. No matter what Larenzo had done, she'd loved this man. For a night.

'Ava,' she said quietly.

'Ava,' he repeated, and she closed her eyes against the wonder she heard in his voice. 'How old is she?'

'Ten months. She was born on Christmas Eve.'

'Would you have ever told me about her?' he asked after a moment.

She opened her eyes and stared at him helplessly. 'Larenzo, you were in *prison*. You were convicted of about a thousand charges all related to being in the Mafia. How could I tell you?'

He gazed back steadily, unmoved by her argument. 'The charges were dropped.'

'I didn't know that. And I still don't know why they were dropped—'

'You still think I'm guilty?' he cut her off, his voice hard.

'I don't *know*,' she cried. 'Larenzo, you have to understand how it was for me. The day you were arrested... those men...'

Even now, a year and a half later, the memory of that night made shame and fear roil through her. 'It was horrible. And then I spent the whole day in the anti-Mafia headquarters in Palermo while they told me you were involved in the Mafia, how they had all this evidence...what was I supposed to believe?'

'Me. You could have believed me.'

'You confessed,' she shot back. 'I read it in the papers. So I did believe you.'

He pressed his lips together, his gaze narrowed and hard. 'Of course you did.'

'And yet you still seem to think I should have believed in your innocence.'

He didn't answer, and Emma bit her lip. She felt cold inside, so terribly cold. For a year and a half she'd been so certain of Larenzo's guilt, and yet now, having seen him only for a few minutes, she felt doubt creep in along with the bittersweet memories. Who was the real man—the Mafia monster or the one she'd made love to?

'But just now,' he finally said. 'You wanted me to leave. Even now, when you knew the charges had been dropped, that I was free, you were trying to keep me from my child.'

'Because as far as I know, you're still a dangerous man,' Emma retorted. Larenzo's eyes narrowed and she almost took a step back. Yet even now she realised she wasn't actually afraid of him. She didn't think he'd hurt her, but...

What was she afraid of, then? Because she certainly felt the cold claws of terror digging into her soul, icing over her mind. 'Even if you are innocent of the charges they laid against you,' she continued more calmly, 'you must have Mafia connections, something that made the police—'

'Not in the way you think,' he bit out, and Emma just shook her head, overwhelmed with too many terrible emotions to respond. 'I am a free man,' Larenzo said in a low voice. 'And you can't keep me from my daughter.'

Emma pressed her hand to her forehead. 'We can't talk about this now,' she said. 'My sister will be home in a few minutes, and Ava is going to wake up soon. I never even expected to see you again, Larenzo. Having you turn up out of the blue...' She shook her head. 'It's a lot to take in.'

'I understand,' he answered levelly. 'But know this. I *will* be back, and I will see Ava again. Don't think for a moment you can keep me from her.'

His mouth compressed and his eyes flashed silver and Emma's stomach did a sickening little flip. She had no idea what to think, to believe.

'We'll talk,' she managed. 'Soon.'

Larenzo held her gaze for an endless, agonising moment, and then with one swift nod he turned and left the room. Emma heard the click of the front door closing and she sagged against the kitchen counter, utterly emotionally spent.

'Emma?' A minute later her sister's voice, lilting with curiosity, floated down the hall. 'Who was that leaving the house?'

Emma straightened as her sister came into the kitchen with Ryan in tow, her eyebrows raised, a smile playing about her mouth. 'Do you have a secret admirer?'

'Hardly.' Emma took a deep breath. 'That was Larenzo Cavelli.'

'What?' The smile slid clear off Meghan's face and numbly Emma explained the events of the last hour. Ava woke up just as she was finishing and she hurried upstairs, grateful for a moment to collect her thoughts, few as she had.

'Mama.' Ava wound her arms around her neck as Emma closed her eyes and breathed in her daughter's scent, baby powder with a hint of the banana she'd eaten for lunch. Ava pressed her cheek against Emma's chest, letting out a snuggly sigh, and Emma's heart gave a painful squeeze. She would do anything for Ava. Anything to keep her safe... even if it meant keeping her from her father.

Yet how could she do that? And should she, if Larenzo were really innocent?

'Ava, sweetheart,' she whispered against the baby's silky hair. 'What are we going to do?'

She stayed upstairs for a few moments, cuddling Ava and then changing her diaper, wanting to put off the conversation she'd have to have with Meghan. Wanting to put off thinking about Larenzo Cavelli and what she was going to do.

Yet even in the dim quiet of her and Ava's bedroom, memories invaded. Memories not of Larenzo as he'd been only moments ago, coldly angry, clearly ruthless, but as he'd been the night their daughter had been conceived. The tenderness he'd shown, as well as the despair. That sorrow and resignation she'd felt in him, had yearned to take away, and the aching, reverent gentleness of his touch...

Remembering that man made all the certainties she'd cultivated over the last eighteen months scatter like ash.

What if he wasn't guilty?

But what if he is?

'Emma?' Meghan's voice was sharp with concern as she called up the stairs. 'Are you coming down?'

'Yes, I'll be there in a moment.' Taking a deep breath, Emma settled Ava on her hip and headed downstairs. Ryan was playing in the playroom adjoining the kitchen and she put Ava on the floor with him, scattering a few blocks and soft toys around. Knowing her daughter as she did, Ava would throw all the toys across the room and then try to grab the trains Ryan was playing with. Her daughter knew what she wanted...just like her father.

'I can't believe Larenzo Cavelli came here,' Meghan said, her voice hollow with shock. She filled up the kettle, shaking her head slowly. 'How did he even know...?'

'The address was on my employment application.'

'And he wants to see Ava?'

'I don't know what he wants exactly, but he told me I couldn't keep him from his daughter.'

Meghan was silent for a moment, her face pale with strain. 'So do you think he is innocent, if the charges were dropped?' she asked and Emma bit her lip.

'I don't know anything any more, Meghan. For a year and a half I thought I knew the truth. I didn't like it, of course, and at times I couldn't believe it, but I thought I *knew.*'

'And now you think you didn't?' Meghan sounded sceptical, and rightly so. How could Emma take anything Larenzo said at face value?

'I don't know. But I suppose I should find out why the

charges against him were dropped.' She reached for the laptop they'd left lying out on the kitchen counter, the browser still on the employment agency's listings. Had it only been a couple of hours ago she'd been worried about what sort of menial job she'd take? It almost seemed laughable.

Quickly Emma typed in the browser's search engine *Larenzo Cavelli charges dropped*. Hundreds of results came up within seconds. She clicked on the first one, and began to read the news article.

All charges have been dropped against convicted felon Larenzo Cavelli when new evidence came to light that business partner Bertrano Raguso was in fact behind the illegal activities...

Meghan peered at the article over her shoulder. 'Do you think it's true?' she asked in a low voice.

'I have no idea.' Emma scanned the rest of the article, skimming over the terrible list of Larenzo's alleged crimes that she'd read in the paper once already. Once had definitely been enough.

'If his business partner really was guilty, why would Larenzo confess?' Meghan asked as she nibbled her lip.

'I don't know.' Emma gazed at the photograph of Bertrano Raguso, a silver-haired man in his sixties, his face set into haggard lines. 'But if they let Larenzo go...'

'But they'd have to, if they have another confession.'

'I don't know if it's that simple.' Emma rubbed her forehead, felt the beginnings of a headache. From the playroom she heard the clatter of blocks being flung across the room, and then Ryan's yowl as one connected with his head. 'I need to see to Ava,' she said. 'I'll have to think about this later. About what I'm going to do.'

'You should consult a lawyer—'

Emma flinched at the thought. She didn't want to get involved in some messy, drawn-out custody battle that would no doubt be splashed across the newspapers, due to Larenzo's notoriety. But what if the alternative was granting him access to Ava? Exposing her to God only knew what kind of danger?

Unless he really was innocent…but how could he not have known about his partner's activities? And why would he have confessed?

Emma let out a tired sigh. Her mind was racing in circles and she knew she had no answers now. 'He might not actually want to be involved with Ava,' she said, trying to convince herself as much as her sister. 'He might just want to see her once…'

'You need to be prepared,' Meghan answered swiftly. 'Emma, the man is—'

'We don't know what he is.'

'Can you really doubt—?'

'I told you, I don't *know*.' And yet if there was any chance Larenzo was guilty, any chance of putting Ava in danger…

'I'll talk to a lawyer,' Emma said. 'I should do that much, at least. Just…just in case.'

Ava and Ryan had both started crying and so Emma scooped her daughter up and distracted her with a few board books before rejoining Meghan at the laptop. Her sister had typed custody lawyers into the search box, and, with her heart thudding sickly and her head still spinning from all that had happened in such a short span of time, Emma watched the results come up, and then she reached for her phone.

CHAPTER SIX

NERVOUSLY EMMA SMOOTHED her hair, straightened her skirt, and then opened the door to the restaurant where she was meeting Larenzo. It had been three endless days since he'd shown up at her sister's house, and Emma had almost started hoping that Larenzo had decided to leave them alone. Yet tangled up in that hope had been an absurd disappointment that he might have given up so easily.

She'd spoken to a lawyer two days ago, and he'd told her that since the charges against Larenzo had been dropped, he would most certainly have a legal right to see Ava. Access could be limited or denied if a court decided there was any danger to her daughter, but it was by no means clear cut or simple.

The next day Larenzo had called and Emma's heart had actually lifted at the sound of his voice. They'd set up a meeting over dinner at a local restaurant, and Emma knew she had no idea what she wanted from this meeting. Her emotions and thoughts were all over the place, and no matter how she tried to order them they raced off in all directions as soon as she thought of Larenzo, remembered how he'd once been with her.

The atmosphere, she saw as she came into the restaurant, was elegant and understated, candlelight flickering over snowy white tablecloths. It almost seemed romantic, which didn't help her disordered thoughts, her clamouring emotions. No matter what she and Larenzo decided about Ava, romance had no place in their lives any more.

She gave her name to the *maître d'* and he showed her to a table in the back, set in a private alcove. Larenzo was already seated, and he rose as she approached. He wore a white button-down shirt and plain grey trousers, and yet he still seemed bigger and darker and more magnetic than any other person in the room.

Once, only once, she'd allowed herself to be drawn by that magnetic force. Now she knew she needed to be immune. To stay strong.

Emma sat down across from him, busying herself with putting her napkin in her lap as Larenzo settled back into his seat, seeming to take up too much space, too much air. Why had it become hard to breathe?

'Thank you for coming,' he said.

Emma took a deep breath, letting the air fill her lungs. 'I didn't really have much choice, did I?'

He pressed his lips together and Emma could almost feel the tension crackle between them. 'This doesn't have to be unpleasant, Emma.'

'And how do you figure that?' she shot back. She'd wanted to stay calm for this meeting but already her composure was cracking, revealing the fear and uncertainty underneath. 'I'm here to discuss a man with Mafia connections being involved with my daughter—'

'*My* daughter,' Larenzo cut across her, his voice low and intense. 'She's my daughter too. Never forget that.'

'Unfortunately, I won't.'

He sat back in his chair, his fingers laced together as he gazed at her. 'Do you hate me?' he asked, as if it was a matter of academic interest, and Emma could only stare at him, flummoxed. *Where had that come from?* 'Because,' he continued, 'you seem as if you hate me.'

'I...' She searched for words, disconcerted by how

much his question had unsettled her. 'I don't hate you,' she said finally. 'I don't feel anything for you.' Which was a bold-faced lie. She didn't know what she felt for Larenzo Cavelli, but it was definitely something. 'But I love my daughter,' she continued shakily, 'and I want to protect her—'

'And you think I don't want that?'

'I don't know what to think about you, Larenzo. I have no idea what to believe.'

'How about the truth?'

'Which is?' she demanded, her voice rising. 'Eighteen months ago you confessed to a long, sordid list of crimes. A week ago, your business partner was convicted of those same crimes, thanks to new evidence, but what am I meant to believe? How on earth do you expect me to trust you?'

Larenzo expelled a long, low breath. 'I don't,' he said flatly. 'You can't trust anyone in this world. That's one thing I've come to realise.'

'Why did you confess if you weren't guilty?'

He pressed his lips together as he flicked his gaze away. 'Because there was overwhelming evidence to convict me.'

'How?'

'Look, I don't want to get into all that now. I left that life behind—'

'And I'm supposed to just *accept* that?'

Larenzo leaned forward, his gaze glittering. 'Emma, do you honestly think I'd put my own child in danger? Do you think I'd be here if I thought I'd be hurting Ava?'

Emma bit her lip. She didn't think that, but she was still afraid. Still reluctant to relinquish control, to let Larenzo into Ava's life. Into her life, in any way at all, and with a jolt she realised it wasn't just because of his possible criminal connections. It was because this man affected her. And she was afraid to let him do that again.

Larenzo leaned back in his chair. 'I left Italy for good

and severed all ties to Cavelli Enterprises. Bertrano Raguso is in prison for the crimes he committed. That is all you need to know.'

'Why New York?' Emma asked. The waiter came forward to take their order, and she gazed blindly at the menu. She had no appetite at all. Finally she picked a relatively plain chicken dish, and Larenzo ordered for himself, before they were left alone again and he answered her question.

'I wanted a new start. Cavelli Enterprises had no holdings in America.'

'What's happened to Cavelli Enterprises?'

'Its assets were seized by the government. Everything's frozen while the investigation continues.'

'So even though there was evidence...?'

Larenzo's mouth hardened into a flat line. 'Bertrano is claiming he is innocent, but the evidence is incontrovertible.' His mouth twisted. 'In the meantime the company will most likely be liquidated, and its remaining assets distributed to shareholders.' He spoke dispassionately, as if it was a matter of indifference to him. Emma searched his face, saw a hardness underneath his bland expression that she didn't think had been there before.

'Were you close to him? This Raguso?'

Larenzo hesitated, one hand resting flat on the tabletop. 'A bit,' he finally said.

'And do you think he did it?'

'I know he did.' He shifted in his chair, his gaze arrowing in on her. 'While I was in prison, my staff investigated and found proof of his guilt. But enough talk of what is past. It's the future that concerns me.'

'The past is important, Larenzo—'

'I've told you all you need to know,' he cut across her. 'I want to talk about Ava.'

She knew it was coming, and yet she still resisted. 'What about her?'

For a second his face softened, his mouth curving into something almost like a smile and just that little look made Emma start to melt. 'What is she like? From the little I saw of her already, it seems like she knows her own mind.'

'She does. She's a force to be reckoned with, that's for sure.'

'Her strength will serve her well later in life.'

'So I keep telling myself.' To her shock Emma realised she was smiling, and Larenzo was actually smiling back.

'I want to see her,' Larenzo said firmly, and Emma took a deep breath.

'There's a playground near the house—'

Larenzo's expression darkened, his eyes flashing silver fire. 'A playground? Do you think you can fob me off with an hour or two at a local park?'

'It's a start, Larenzo—'

'I've missed the first ten months of my daughter's life. I want to spend time with her, Emma. Real time. Not be introduced to her as if I'm some stranger in a park playground.'

Emma stared down at the table, conscious of how quickly Larenzo had torn apart her suggestion. She'd wanted to stage-manage his entrance into Ava's life, to exert some control over the proceedings, and hopefully to limit them. She should have known Larenzo wouldn't let her do that. He was a man who was in control. Always.

'Very well.' She took a deep, even breath and let it out slowly. 'What do you suggest?'

'I've taken an apartment in New York, and it has plenty of room. I suggest you and Ava move there with me.'

Emma gaped at him, stunned into silence for a few seconds. 'You want me to move in with you?' she finally managed, her voice ending in something close to a squeak.

'I'm not suggesting we have some sort of relationship,' Larenzo clarified coolly. 'I have no interest in that. But I want to see my daughter as much as possible, and be a real presence in her life. Your current living arrangements are neither sustainable nor suitable.' He lifted one powerful shoulder in a shrug. 'The answer seems obvious.'

'To you, maybe.' Emma nearly choked. She shook her head and reached for her glass of water. She'd never expected Larenzo to suggest something like this. To live with him...*to be that near to temptation*...

'I don't see an alternative,' Larenzo answered. 'I want unlimited access to my daughter—'

'Unlimited? Larenzo, be reasonable—' At the very most she'd thought she'd have to have some kind of joint custody arrangement with Larenzo. But this?

This was dangerous. Impossible. *Tempting*...

'I don't really see what the problem is,' Larenzo replied calmly. 'Surely you agree it's better for Ava to have two interested and loving parents in her life?'

Emma swallowed. 'Yes, but that doesn't mean we have to live together—'

'What, precisely, do you object to?' Larenzo asked. His voice had gone quiet, dangerously so. 'You'll have your own room, your own bathroom, and your quarters will be far more comfortable than they are currently.'

Emma stared at him helplessly. He made it all sound so simple, and yet it wasn't. It couldn't be. 'Everything's changed so quickly,' she finally said. 'I can't process it all—'

'Then take your time,' Larenzo answered. 'You have until tomorrow.'

'*Tomorrow*—'

'I want to see my daughter, Emma.'

'I know you do.' Except she hadn't expected Larenzo to feel this strongly, this *fiercely*, about his role as a father. That he did surprised her, but she realised she couldn't resent it. She knew what it was like to have a parent who chose a life without you. Who walked away from her child.

Despite all the obstacles, all the unknowns, she realised she was, amazingly, glad Larenzo wanted to be involved… even if she was scared about what it meant.

'I can't just *live* with you,' she finally burst out.

Larenzo arched an eyebrow, all arrogant assurance. 'Why not?'

'Because…because…' Because she was afraid of this man, and it had nothing to do with any criminal connections. She was afraid of his power over her, her need for him. 'I need to have my own life, Larenzo. I was planning on moving out of my sister's house for that reason. I'm twenty-seven years old and I'm not going to freeload off people for ever.'

'So this is a question of money?'

'Not just money,' she returned. 'It's about independence and autonomy. I need to be my own person—'

'And you can't do that living in my apartment?' He made her feel ridiculous, and yet she *couldn't* just fall in with his plans, fit into his life without having one of her own.

'I can't believe I'm even thinking of moving in with you,' she said, shaking her head slowly.

'It makes sense.'

Emma didn't answer. It *did* make a certain kind of bizarre sense, which both aggravated and alarmed her. Three days ago she'd thought Larenzo Cavelli would spend his life in prison. Two days ago she would have fought tooth and nail to keep him out of her daughter's life.

And now she was thinking of living with him? She pressed her fingers to her temples and closed her eyes. 'This is so crazy.'

'Maybe so,' Larenzo agreed with a shrug, 'but it's our reality. I won't take no for an answer, Emma.'

She opened her eyes and stared at him, saw that coldness in his eyes, the hint of how hard he could be. 'What would you do if I did say no, Larenzo?'

'It won't come to that.'

'But if it did?'

He hesitated, then stated flatly, 'I'd sue for custody.'

Emma jerked back, appalled. 'So this is basically black-mail.'

'No.'

'Then what would you call it? "Live with me or I'll take your child." That's what you're saying, Larenzo.'

'And what are you saying?' he answered, a hint of anger in his voice. '"You're my child's father and I don't want you involved in her life," even though you know I am innocent.'

'I didn't say that—'

'You've been saying that for ten months, Emma.'

She took a deep breath. Arguing would get them no-where. 'Things have changed, Larenzo. I recognise that. But you can't expect me to fall in with your plans without a second's thought—'

'I haven't. I told you, you have until tomorrow.'

'Well, thanks for that,' she answered sarcastically. There was no reasoning with this man. No swaying him. So what was she going to do?

The waiter came with their meals, giving Emma a few minutes' respite from the intensity of their conversation.

She picked at her chicken, her gaze lowered; she didn't think she could swallow a single mouthful. Then, to her shock, she felt Larenzo's hand on her own, his palm warm and strong just as it had been a year and a half ago, when he'd covered her hand with his own and she'd felt, for a moment, closer to this man than anyone else on earth.

'Why are you fighting this, Emma?' he asked quietly, and his voice was as sorrowful as it had been back on that night. His touch and his words catapulted her to that time when she'd felt so much for this man, had longed to com-fort him. Had seen tenderness and understanding in his eyes, had felt it in his arms.

A lump rose in her throat and she blinked rapidly, swallowed past it. 'I don't know,' she whispered, and it sounded like a confession.

'I want to be with Ava. I never had a family of my own, except...' He stopped, his voice choking, and shook his head. 'I don't want this to be acrimonious, God knows. I want to get to know my daughter and love her. Please let me do that.'

She gazed up at him, saw the sincerity and emotion in his eyes, and felt her last reservations melt away. She believed Larenzo. She believed he was innocent, but, more importantly, she believed he wanted what was best for Ava.

She only hoped it was best for her too.

CHAPTER SEVEN

'I CAN'T BELIEVE you're doing this.'

Meghan stood behind Emma as she finished packing her suitcases—just one for her and one for Ava, really not much at all to bring to her new home. Her new life.

'It makes sense, Meghan,' she said, which was what Larenzo had said to her last night. Last night she'd lain in bed, staring at the ceiling, unable to sleep as she'd thought about her future, when she'd heard Meghan's and Pete's raised voices downstairs, and had known they were talking about her. She'd crept to the top of the stairs, everything in her stilling as Pete had declared,

'She can't stay here any longer, Meghan. I've been patient, God knows, but two more mouths to feed is expensive, and if this Cavelli character has connections to—'

'He was cleared of all charges,' Meghan had cut across her husband.

'Even so—'

'She doesn't have anywhere else to go, Pete.'

'Then she needs to find somewhere,' Pete had answered grimly, and Emma had crept back to her bed.

Pete was right. She couldn't stay here any longer, for too many reasons. And she no longer wanted to deny Larenzo access to his daughter, even if she was afraid of what that might mean. Not for Ava, but for her.

'You could stay here,' Meghan persisted, and Emma met her sister's eye in the mirror hanging over the bureau.

'You know I couldn't,' she said quietly, and Meghan flushed and looked away.

'I was afraid you might have heard that conversation—'

'Pete's right, Meghan.'

Meghan bit her lip. 'I like having you here, Emma. You've been away for so long—'

'New York City isn't that far. I'll visit lots, I promise.'

'I'll worry. I still don't trust Cavelli. Even if he was cleared of charges...'

'What happened to innocent until proven guilty?' Emma asked lightly. 'I trust him, Meghan, and I know he wouldn't hurt his daughter.' She paused, her gaze on the clothes she was folding. 'He was good to me when I worked for him.' She bit her lip as a pang of bittersweet longing assailed her. 'He was very good to me.'

'But can you really trust him?' Meghan persisted, and Emma thought of what he'd said last night at dinner. *You can't trust anyone in this world. That's one thing I've come to realise.* When had he realised that? When he was a child at the orphanage, or when he'd been sent to a prison for crimes he might not have committed? A lifetime of betrayal, perhaps, and yet there was still so much she didn't understand.

'Yes, I can,' she answered Meghan. 'At least when it comes to Ava.'

Twenty minutes later Larenzo pulled up in front of Meghan's house in a luxury sedan, a car seat already installed in the centre of the back seat. He loaded the two suitcases in the boot, glancing at Emma.

'That's all you have?'

'I travel light.'

'But Ava—'

'The crib and changing table and things belonged to Meghan. They're hoping for another baby someday, so...'

'You don't need to worry about any of that,' Larenzo said. 'I've taken care of it.'

'Okay,' she murmured, and Larenzo held out his arms for Ava.

'May I?'

Wordlessly she nodded and handed him their daughter. He held her awkwardly, clearly not used to the chubby bundle of arms and legs that was an almost toddler. 'Hello, sweetheart,' he murmured, smiling into Ava's inquisitive face. She gurgled and grabbed his chin in her chubby fists and Larenzo laughed, the sound rusty and surprising and also achingly wonderful. Emma realised she hadn't heard Larenzo laugh before. It reminded her of the photo she'd shown him, back in Sicily; it was a sound of joy. Suddenly she felt almost near tears. She swallowed hard and watched as Larenzo buckled Ava into her car seat; he fiddled with the straps and with a laugh that managed to clear the tears away Emma helped him.

'These things are impossible,' she said. 'Especially when Ava is resisting.' She buckled the straps over Ava's tummy, conscious of Larenzo standing so close to her, his head bent near hers. She closed her eyes, willed herself to develop a little strength. A lot of resistance. Otherwise she was going to have way too many difficult moments with Larenzo. 'There.' She patted the buckled straps and straightened, her breast brushing against Larenzo's arm as she did so. Desire shot through her veins and she quickly turned away and got in the car, deeply unsettled by her own reaction to this man who had catapulted so suddenly back into her life.

Larenzo started the car; Emma was in the passenger seat, her face turned towards the window. He had no idea what she was thinking, if she still resented his presence in Ava's life.

He'd told Emma he didn't trust anyone, and, while that

was true, he was conscious of how he was asking her to trust him with the most precious thing of all: their child. But he also knew he couldn't change who he was, who he'd become. Trust was now an alien concept, and always would be. Even so, he could appreciate what Emma was doing.

'Thank you,' he said abruptly, and she turned to him warily.

'For what?' she asked and he cleared his throat.

'For agreeing to live with me.'

'When the alternative is having you sue me for custody,' she answered after a moment, 'there wasn't really any question, was there?'

Guilt needled him at the realisation of how effectively he'd blackmailed her. Was he really any better than Bertrano, when he resorted to such tactics? And yet Emma would have denied him his own flesh and blood, the child he'd never expected to have, the family he'd longed for since he was a child himself.

'Well,' he said after a moment, 'I'm still grateful.' Emma did not reply.

They drove in silence for the entire hour's journey into the city; Ava babbled and gurgled in the back seat, and by the time they approached the Lincoln Tunnel she was tired of the car and began to protest, straining against the straps of her car seat.

Emma tried to distract her with a few toys and then a rice cake, all of which entertained Ava for about three seconds before she hurled each item to the floor.

'Sorry,' Emma said as she glanced down at the floor of the back seat. 'You have a sea of rice cake crumbs down there.'

'It doesn't matter.'

'Are you sure you're prepared for this?' she asked as Ava drummed her heels against the seat. 'Ava is a force to be reckoned with.'

'So I can see—and hear,' Larenzo answered dryly. 'I don't know if I'm prepared. But I'm willing to take it on.' She need never doubt him in that.

'Did you ever want children?' Emma asked. 'I mean, before…'

'Before I went to prison?' Larenzo filled in flatly. 'I don't know if I really thought of it. I didn't have time for a relationship.'

'Yet you've certainly had your share of women.'

His mouth tightened as he slid her a sideways glance. She'd spoken without expression, and he had no idea what she thought of that aspect of his past. Not that it actually mattered, since there would never be anything like that between them. He had nothing to offer Emma, or anyone. Not in that way. 'I don't deny it,' he said after a moment.

'Having a baby in your apartment, as well as her mother, might cramp your style a bit.'

Larenzo shook his head. 'I've no interest in anything like that any more.'

Emma raised her eyebrows, clearly sceptical. 'Larenzo, you're what? In your mid-thirties? Surely you're going to want a woman again.'

Want a woman. The last woman he'd been with had been Emma, and he'd wanted her almost unbearably. Just remembering the sweetness of her touch, the innocent and utter yielding of her body when he'd needed her so badly, made lust shaft through him with a sudden, painful intensity.

He shifted as discreetly as he could in his seat and kept his eyes on the road. He might have told Emma he wasn't interested in relationships or sex any more, and in truth his libido had disappeared while he'd been in prison, along with all of his other feelings and desires. But he could feel it returning in force now.

'What about you?' he asked. 'You might meet someone.' A thought that he disliked instinctively, although he knew he had no right to.

'I can't even imagine meeting someone,' Emma said with a small sigh. 'Ava takes up all my energy.'

'She won't be a baby for ever.'

'No,' Emma said slowly. 'But, Larenzo, this…situation can't last for ever.'

He turned to her sharply, his eyes narrowed. 'What do you mean?'

'I can't live with you for ever. I accept that it's expedient for now, and of course it gives you time to get to know her, but eventually…I need my own life. You'll need yours. When Ava is a little older, we can come to a custody arrangement we can both live with.'

Larenzo didn't answer for a moment. He knew she was talking sense but everything in him rebelled against it. Ava was the only family he'd ever had. He wasn't going to give her up, not even in part, as easily as that.

'We'll discuss the future when it is relevant,' he said, making his tone final. They'd driven through the Lincoln Tunnel and now came out into midtown Manhattan, all of them blinking in the bright sunlight. Even Ava had stopped protesting against the hated car seat as she gazed curiously at the gleaming skyscrapers and the streets teeming with people.

Emma turned to stare out of the window, and Larenzo saw she looked almost as wide-eyed as her daughter. 'Have you spent much time in New York before?'

'Not really. As a kid I always lived abroad. My apartment is on the Central Park West, right near the Natural History Museum. It's a good area for children.'

'You've only been in America for a week, haven't you?' Emma asked. 'How did you manage to secure an apartment so quickly?'

'Money talks.'

'And even though the assets of Cavelli Enterprises are frozen, you have money?'

'I had my own savings, which were released to me when the charges were cleared.'

She turned to give him a direct look. 'Are you ever going to tell me the whole story, Larenzo?'

His hands tensed on the steering wheel and he stared straight ahead as he navigated the roundabout at Columbus Circle. 'I've told you what you need to know, Emma.' Perhaps it was foolish to keep the truth from her about Bertrano; it was shaming that he still felt a loyalty to a man who, despite years of shared history, of happy memories, had completely and utterly betrayed him. And he knew that telling Emma his part of the story, how he'd been duped and deceived, wouldn't make much difference. Yet it would make a difference to him. He didn't want to admit how naive he'd been, how *hurt* he'd been. Not to Emma. Not to anyone.

And maybe Emma sensed some of what he felt, for to Larenzo's surprise she laid a hand on his arm, the touch of her fingers as light as a butterfly's. 'I hope you will be able to tell me someday, Larenzo. For your sake as much as mine.'

They didn't talk after that until Larenzo had pulled up to the elegant brick building that faced Central Park. A valet came out to deal with the car, and a doorman went for their bags.

Larenzo turned to get Ava out of her car seat; she practically flung herself into his arms and Larenzo held his daughter to him, breathing in her clean baby scent as her dark hair tickled his face. *His daughter.* Even now he nearly reeled from the shock and force of that knowledge. He had a family.

'Do you want me to take her?' Emma asked, reaching for Ava, and Larenzo shook his head.

'She's okay with me.' Although he wasn't so sure about that when Ava began to flail, scrambling to get down.

Emma laughed and reached for her, and reluctantly Larenzo gave Ava over to her. 'I guess she wants her mother.'

'Actually, I think she just wants to crawl all over this marble floor and get really dirty,' Emma answered lightly. She smiled at him, and he thought he saw sympathy in her eyes. 'She'll get used to you.'

He nodded, his throat too tight for words. He'd thought he had nothing left inside him; he'd been sure he was broken and empty inside. But knowing he had a daughter, knowing he could have someone to love and be loved by, filled him up to overflowing.

Emma followed Larenzo into the sumptuous foyer of the apartment building, all marble floors and glittering chandeliers. A doorman nodded respectfully to Larenzo as they passed, and then they stepped into a large wood-panelled lift, complete with a sofa and gilt mirror.

'Fancy,' Emma murmured as they soared upwards to the penthouse and then stepped into the huge foyer of Larenzo's apartment.

'This marble is a bit hard for a baby,' she said, tapping the black and white chequered marble with one foot. 'I wouldn't want Ava to fall and hurt herself.'

'I'll arrange to have it carpeted immediately,' Larenzo answered without missing a beat, and Emma wondered if she'd been challenging him. How far would Larenzo go to accommodate his daughter? Did she even want to answer that question?

She felt a churning mix of emotions as she stepped into the living room, its large windows overlooking Central Park, now ablaze in autumn colours. On one hand, she was grateful that Larenzo was interested in his daughter. How could she not be? And yet she was also afraid. Afraid of the darkness of his past, the secrets he wasn't telling her. But more than that: she was afraid of feeling too much for him, of getting too used to this. To him. Of caring for a man who had no intention of reciprocating her feelings. Surely she wouldn't be so weak. She wouldn't let herself.

'Would you like to come see the nursery?' Larenzo asked, coming to stand behind her at the window, Ava in his arms.

Emma turned. 'There's a nursery?'

'I had it all delivered yesterday.'

Wordlessly she nodded and followed Larenzo down the luxuriously carpeted hall to the bedrooms.

'My bedroom is here,' he said, indicating a door on the left. 'And your bedroom is here.' He pointed to a door directly across from his. 'The nursery is adjoining yours. I thought you'd prefer that.'

'I do,' Emma said, although the thought of having her own bedroom after ten months of sharing cramped quarters with her daughter was a luxury she intended to enjoy. 'Thank you,' she added belatedly, and Larenzo just nodded as he opened the door to the nursery.

She'd been expecting something basic and expedient, ordered and set up in a hurry, but the room she stepped into looked as if it had taken months of planning. The walls were painted a pale lilac, and matching curtains framed the deep window that overlooked the park. Deeper purple accents were scattered around the room: a throw pillow on the rocking chair, a silk-patterned lampshade, a close-up photograph of a violet on the wall. It was a lovely, creative room that was perfect for a baby without being cloyingly sweet or infantile.

'I thought you might like something other than the standard pink,' Larenzo said, and Emma heard a surprising note of uncertainty, even vulnerability, in his voice. 'But of course if you don't like it, you must change it. You can redecorate anything in the apartment as you like.'

'I don't want to redecorate,' Emma answered honestly. 'I love it. It's perfect, Larenzo. Thank you.'

'Good.'

Emma set Ava down on the plush carpet and she crawled towards a purple rocking horse—actually, Emma saw, a unicorn with a glittery horn—set in the corner, reaching up to grasp the handles as she pulled herself to standing.

'She's clever, isn't she?' Larenzo said with pride. 'She'll be walking soon.'

'And then there will really be no stopping her.' Emma gazed round the room again, noting all the unique touches. 'So did you hire an interior decorator?' she asked, and Larenzo shook his head.

'No, I did it myself. I enjoyed picking out all the things.'

'It must have taken an age—'

'No, just an afternoon. I hired painters to come and do the walls, and I put the furniture together myself.' He paused and then added, 'I told you I wanted to be involved, Emma.'

'I know, but...' She shook her head, overwhelmed by the thought and consideration Larenzo had clearly put into the nursery. She pictured him with an instruction leaflet and a set of tools, laboriously putting the crib and changing table together, and felt as if a fist had clenched around her heart. 'I suppose I didn't really think you'd be a hands-on dad,' she confessed, and Larenzo raised his eyebrows.

'Why not?'

'I don't know. You were so busy with work when I was your housekeeper. You hardly had time to come to the villa. And your lifestyle...'

'Things are different now.'

'Yes.' Emma swallowed, trying to banish the images

that had sprung into her mind, memories of the last night Larenzo had come to the villa, had come to her. She had to put that behind her. Heaven knew Larenzo had. 'Yes,' she repeated more firmly. 'Things are different now.'

CHAPTER EIGHT

AFTER SETTLING AVA in her new crib for an afternoon nap, Emma went to her bedroom and began to unpack her few possessions. She could hear Larenzo moving around in his bedroom across the hall, and the closeness of the quarters made her feel…aware.

She was still overwhelmingly attracted to Larenzo. It was a fact she had to acknowledge, and perhaps acknowledging it would help her to deal with it. Larenzo had made it abundantly clear that he had no interest in her that way any more, and she didn't even want him to. At least, she *shouldn't* want him to. Emma let out a rueful sigh as she acknowledged the truth—and strength—of her feelings. But she also knew their relationship, if they even had one, was way too complicated already.

And yet the tenderness he'd shown with Ava, the consideration he'd shown her…they chipped away at her defences. Made her remember. Made her want things she had absolutely no business wanting.

She might believe in Larenzo's innocence, but that didn't mean he was *safe*.

Ava was still sleeping after she'd unpacked, and so Emma headed out to the living room. The room was spacious and luxuriously appointed, if a little bland. No personal photographs or mementoes, but then Larenzo had bought the place only a week ago. It had probably come furnished.

She prowled around the room, glancing at the antique vases, the gilt mirrors, feeling restless and not quite knowing why.

She gazed out of the window at the leafy enclave of Central Park and as she imagined taking Ava to one of the playgrounds there, exploring the city with her daughter, her spirits lifted a little. She could make this work. She had to make this work, at least for a little while.

'Was your room adequate?'

Emma spun around to see Larenzo standing in the doorway of the sitting room. He'd changed from his more casual clothes of this morning to a well-tailored suit in navy-blue silk, and he looked, as he always did, devastatingly attractive. Even from across the room Emma felt the force of his magnetism, and it nearly propelled her forward, towards him. She held onto the window sill for balance as she answered him.

'Yes, thank you. More than adequate. This is a beautiful apartment, Larenzo.'

'You must change anything you don't like.'

She thought of telling him she wouldn't be staying long enough to warrant such changes, but somehow she couldn't make herself say the words. She just nodded instead, and Larenzo turned towards the door.

'I have to go out now, for some business meetings, but I should be back this evening.'

'Okay.' Emma wasn't sure why this surprised her, but it did. What had she expected—she and Larenzo would spend the day together? Larenzo had made it clear they would be living separate lives, brought together only by Ava, which was how she wanted it. How she had to want it. 'Do you—do you want me to make something for dinner?' She saw surprise flash across Larenzo's face and she wondered if she'd pushed some undiscussed boundary, crossed some invisible line. Maybe Larenzo had no intention of eating with her or Ava. She had no idea how this was meant to work, how it was going to work.

'If it's no trouble, that would be fine,' he finally said.

'It's no trouble.'

With a nod of farewell, Larenzo left the apartment and Emma stood there for a moment, feeling the emptiness all around her, not able to decide if she was relieved he had gone...or disappointed.

She made her way to the kitchen, which was huge, a hymn to granite and stainless steel, with every possible kitchen gadget and appliance. There was, however, no food. She stared into the empty depths of the enormous sub-zero fridge and wondered what Larenzo had been eating for the last few days.

When Ava woke a little while later Emma buckled her daughter into the top-of-the-line stroller that she found in the foyer.

Outside on Central Park West, a brisk autumn breeze blowing and Ava thankfully distracted by all the sights and sounds around them, Emma headed towards Columbus Avenue and the local shops. She felt better with every step she took, the city's vibrant life seeming to infuse her with energy and purpose.

At a local grocery she bought all the ingredients for lasagne, a simple but warming meal on this cold autumn day. She paused in front of a wine shop and then recklessly bought a bottle of Chianti to go with it. She'd already pushed the boundaries of their arrangement by suggesting she cook for Larenzo. Why not own it?

This was her life, at least for now, and she wanted to enjoy it. Ava started getting restless in the stroller, so Emma headed back. Once she was up in the apartment she brought the groceries into the kitchen and settled Ava onto the floor with a few wooden spoons and copper pans. While her daughter made as much noise as she possibly could, Emma bustled around, assembling the lasagne and tossing a salad.

She started to relax as she worked; she'd always enjoyed cooking, and it actually felt good to be mistress of her own kitchen, instead of an interloper in Meghan's. As much as her sister had made her feel welcome, Emma had been conscious of how much of an imposition she really was. Here, at least, she had a job to do, a potential role. Perhaps she could act as Larenzo's housekeeper. It would be a way of earning her keep and making herself useful.

She was just sliding the lasagne out of the oven when Larenzo appeared in the doorway of the kitchen. He'd taken off his suit jacket and loosened his tie, and his jaw was darkened with five o'clock shadow, all of it making him look deliciously rumpled and sexy.

He paused, taking in the sight of the kitchen, and Emma realised what a mess it was, with pots and spoons all over the floor for Ava's entertainment, and the detritus from her cooking all over the counters.

'Sorry, I'm not very good at cleaning up as I cook,' she said.

'No, it's fine.' Larenzo glanced around the room again, and Emma couldn't tell anything from his expression. 'I like it,' he said at last. 'Shall I set the table?'

He was already getting the forks and knives from the drawer, and Emma watched him, a strange pressure building in her chest. This was all so…normal. So cosy.

Ava had noticed her father and abandoned her pots and spoons to crawl over to him and pull herself up, clutching his legs. Larenzo glanced down at her, his whole face softening into a smile that made that pressure in Emma's chest turn painful.

'I'm afraid she's dented a few of your pots and pans,' she said stiltedly, turning her gaze to the salad she was needlessly tossing. 'She doesn't know her own strength.'

'I don't mind.' Larenzo scooped Ava up with one hand, settling her on his hip as he took the cutlery to the table in the dining nook of the kitchen. 'This is a bit more manageable than the dining room,' he said as he laid the table. 'I think the table in there seats twenty.'

'Planning on having any dinner parties?'

'No. I don't think I know twenty people who would come to a dinner party I hosted, unless it was to gawp and gossip.' He spoke tonelessly, without self-pity, and Emma eyed him curiously as she brought the lasagne to the table.

'You don't have many friends in America?'

'I don't have many friends, full stop,' Larenzo answered. 'A stint in prison shows you who your true friends are, and mine turned out to be rather few.'

He tried to put Ava in the high chair he'd brought to the table, but the toddler shrieked and arched her back, sticking her legs straight out. Emma watched, amused, as Larenzo tried his best before looking up with a wry smile.

'She's really quite strong.'

'Yes, and she doesn't like being strapped in.' Emma plucked Ava from the chair and put her back down on the floor. 'She'll want to join us when we sit down.'

'I suppose I have a lot to learn.'

'Fortunately Ava provides a steep learning curve,' Emma answered with a smile.

Emma brought the meal to the table and they both sat down. Just as she'd predicted, Ava crawled over to them, wanting to be part of things.

Larenzo glanced down at his daughter, smiling when she lifted her arms for him to pick her up. He settled her in her high chair this time without Ava making any protest. 'Tell me about the last ten months,' he said to Emma when he'd sat down again. 'Or even before that. How was your pregnancy?'

'Mostly uneventful, thankfully,' Emma answered. 'I

was pretty nauseous for the first three months,' she continued. 'But then it settled down. She was quite the kicker, though. I couldn't sleep most nights because it felt like she was playing football inside of me.'

Larenzo smiled at that, his whole face lightening, and Emma quickly looked down at her plate. Larenzo's smile was dangerous.

'And the birth? It went well?'

'As well as these things go,' Emma answered frankly. 'It hurt. A lot.'

'Why didn't you get pain relief?'

'No time. She came a week early; she wasn't due until New Year's Eve. And I didn't think I could actually be in labour, because the contractions were irregular and they didn't hurt all that much.' She let out a sudden, embarrassed laugh. 'I can't believe I'm telling you all this.'

'Why not? I want to hear it.'

'Really?' She heard the scepticism in her voice, and Larenzo must have too, because he nodded firmly.

'Absolutely. I missed this, Emma. I want to know now.'

But would he have wanted to know then? If Larenzo hadn't gone to prison, would he have been an involved father? Would they be dating or even *married* now? Emma's cheeks heated at the thought. She was glad Larenzo had no idea the turn her thoughts had taken. She cleared her throat and continued. 'Well, Meghan had been telling me how first babies take for ever, and as it was Christmas Eve I was hoping the contractions might die down. I didn't want to be in the hospital over Christmas.'

'Understandable.'

'But they didn't, and by the time I realised we needed to go to the hospital, Ava was almost ready to make her arrival.' She smiled at the memory. 'Meghan was pushing me in a wheelchair into the delivery ward, and I was bellowing at the top of my lungs. I'm not so good with pain.'

'I wish I could have been there,' Larenzo said quietly, and Emma knew he meant it.

Before she could think better of it, she asked the question that had been dancing through her mind. 'What do you suppose would have happened, if you hadn't gone to prison?'

Larenzo frowned. 'What do you mean?'

'I would have stayed on as your housekeeper. I would have told you I was pregnant right away.' She held her breath, waiting for him to say something, although she didn't know what.

Larenzo sighed and leaned back in his chair. 'The truth is, Emma, if I hadn't gone to prison, if I hadn't known I was going to go to prison, there wouldn't have been a baby. That night happened because I knew I was going to be arrested in the morning.'

'Oh.' Emma blinked, stupidly feeling hurt by this, and not quite sure what to do with that emotion. 'I see.'

'You gave me something precious that night.'

'My virginity?' she filled in, trying to joke, but it came out flat.

'No, I didn't mean that, although that of course is precious too.'

She really didn't want to be having this conversation. She kept looking at her plate, focusing on the food she no longer felt like eating.

'I meant comfort,' Larenzo said quietly. 'Human connection. Pleasure, not just physical pleasure, although there certainly was that. But pleasure in talking to you, and being in your company. Playing chess, seeing your photographs… that night made a memory that sustained me through many dark days in prison.'

'Oh.' And now she didn't feel so hurt. She felt…*honoured* that she'd been that important to him, and deeply thankful that their one night together had meant something to him, as it had to her. 'Well, I'm glad about that, I suppose.'

'And look at the result.' He glanced at Ava, who now had tomato sauce in her hair, before turning back to Emma with a smile. 'I don't have any regrets, since she came out of it. But I think she needs a bath.'

'Do you want me to—?' Emma half rose from her chair as Larenzo unbuckled Ava from her high chair.

'I can do it,' he said.

'She can be pretty tricky in the tub—'

As if to prove her point, Ava started wriggling out of Larenzo's grasp, and soon his shirt was splattered with tomato sauce.

Larenzo looked rather endearingly amazed by his daughter's gymnastics and Emma rescued him. 'I've found this is the best way sometimes,' she said, and, tucking Ava under her arm as if she were a parcel, she took her to the bathroom.

Larenzo followed, standing in the doorway while Emma put Ava down and turned the taps on. 'Fortunately she likes her bath,' she said, and turned to look over her shoulder. Her breath dried in her throat as she saw he was unbuttoning his shirt. What, she wondered distantly, was so mesmerising about his long brown fingers sliding buttons out of their holes? Something was, because she couldn't tear her gaze away from the sight.

'I'd rather not get my shirt wet,' Larenzo explained. 'I have a feeling Ava is a splasher.' He shrugged out of his dress shirt, revealing a plain white T-shirt underneath that clung to the defined muscles of his chest and abdomen.

'She is,' Emma answered, and finally managed to drag her gaze to Larenzo's face. She couldn't read the emotion in his eyes, and she hoped that he hadn't noticed how she'd been staring. *Wanting.*

She knew she should go back to the kitchen and clean

up their dishes, but she felt as if her feet were rooted to the floor, and all she could do was watch as Larenzo battled Ava out of her clothes and then plopped her in the tub, one strong hand resting on her back to keep her steady.

'Is this right?' he asked, and the uncertainty in his voice made Emma's heart ache.

'Yes…yes, that's perfect.' She felt as if her feelings were a kaleidoscope that Larenzo twirled every time he spoke. In these unguarded moments of honesty everything in her swelled with feeling, ached with loss.

What if things could have been different? What if that night *had* still happened, without the arrest, and she and Larenzo had built a relationship? What if they'd become a proper family, rather than this awkwardly constructed temporary one?

Emma knew she shouldn't torment herself with such thoughts. She'd never been looking for that kind of relationship, and, in any case, there was no going back. And yet as she gazed helplessly at Larenzo bathing their daughter, she almost wished there were.

Half an hour later Emma had cleaned up the kitchen when Larenzo emerged from the nursery with Ava in her pyjamas.

'You've buttoned up her pyjamas wrong,' she remarked in amusement as Larenzo raked a hand through his hair.

'Those things are worse than a straitjacket. There are a million buttons.'

'It's a learned skill.'

'Clearly.' He pulled his damp T-shirt away from his chest, and Emma tried not to stare at his perfect musculature, or remember how warm and satiny his skin had felt, how she'd once put her lips to his taut abdomen…

'She's ready for bed, I think,' Emma said. 'I'll get her bottle ready.' She'd brought a can of infant formula from Meghan's, and now she poured cooled boiled water into a bottle and added a few scoops of the white powder. 'You were a little low on groceries, by the way,' she said. 'I don't think there's anything for breakfast.'

'I can arrange for food to be delivered, unless you'd prefer to do it yourself.'

'Actually, I was thinking about that,' Emma said. She'd finished making the bottle and Ava was reaching for it with both hands. 'I'm not comfortable just living off your generosity, and one thing I know how to do is be a house-keeper.'

Larenzo stilled. 'What are you suggesting?'

'I could be your housekeeper. You don't have to pay me, but at least it will make up for mine and Ava's room and board.'

Larenzo's face had darkened as she spoke. 'Ava is my daughter, Emma, and you are her mother. This isn't a question of *room and board.*'

Emma took a deep breath, knowing she needed to say this even if part of her didn't want to. 'It is for me, Larenzo.' He didn't answer and she continued, keeping her voice steady with effort, 'Look, you said yourself you aren't interested in a relationship. You want to get to know Ava, and I respect that. But the only reason I'm here is because Ava is. So it makes sense for me to have a role. A job.'

Still Larenzo didn't speak, and Emma could see the emotions battling on his face. She just didn't know what they were. Did he want there to be more between them? Or was that just her foolish, wishful thinking? Sighing, she hoisted Ava more firmly on her hip. 'I'm going to put her to bed. Think about it, at least.'

She was at the door when Larenzo finally bit out, 'Fine, you can act as housekeeper. But I don't want any respon-sibilities you needlessly put on yourself to take away from Ava's care.'

'Many women manage a home and a baby,' Emma answered, doing her best to keep her voice mild. 'I think I can too.' Larenzo said nothing and as she headed to the nursery with Ava, Emma wondered why this didn't feel more like a victory.

CHAPTER NINE

ANOTHER SLEEPLESS NIGHT. By now Larenzo was well used to insomnia. He'd slept badly in prison, on a thin mattress in a tiny cell with a thousand other prisoners shifting, coughing, and groaning around him. Ironic that he slept just as badly now that he was free, lying on a king-sized bed with the apartment quiet and still.

And Emma sleeping across the hall.

Although he knew he shouldn't, he imagined rising from his bed, opening his door, and going into Emma's room. Watching her sleep, her golden-brown hair spread across the pillow, her lithe body clad in those scanty pyjamas he remembered from their night in Sicily.

Then he imagined sliding into that bed with her, taking her in his arms, burying his face in her sweet-smelling hair, burying himself inside her body…

With a groan Larenzo rose from the bed and went to the en-suite bathroom to splash some cold water on his face. He had no business thinking of Emma that way. His libido might have leapt to life since he'd seen her again, but he had nothing left in his heart to give her. No ability to have a relationship, to trust or to love someone.

He loved Ava, because she was sweet and innocent, and she was his. His love for his daughter was rock solid, utterly unshakeable. But loving a woman? Trusting someone with the heart that had shattered into tiny fragments of nothingness?

Impossible.

And the alternative, some kind of fling or affair, would only further complicate what was already a tenuous arrangement. His face settled into a scowl as he thought of Emma's suggestion. *Housekeeper.* He didn't want her here as a housekeeper. She wasn't his damned employee. She was here because she was the mother of his child, because she *belonged*—

Larenzo let out his breath in a hiss as he bowed his head. Emma belonged with Ava, but not with him. Not like that. Never like that.

So perhaps, much as he had instinctively disliked the idea, it was better that she act as housekeeper. Perhaps having a clearly defined role would help them navigate this arrangement with a minimum of awkwardness.

A soft cry interrupted the wrangling of his own thoughts and Larenzo realised that Ava had woken up. Quickly he left his room and went to the nursery. His daughter was standing up in her crib, her face streaked with tears. Larenzo's heart twisted with a powerful mixture of love, protectiveness, and sorrow. Sleeping in a strange place had to be a frightening experience for the child.

He picked her up, and again his heart twisted as Ava settled against his bare chest, her cheek resting over his heart. Larenzo stroked her back and without even realising what he was doing, he began to croon a lullaby in Italian. *'E dormi, dormi, dormi, bambin de cuna. To mama no la gh'è la a-sé andà via.'*

The words came to him unbidden, from a deep well of memory. He stroked Ava's hair and watched as his daughter's eyelids eventually drooped.

After several minutes when he was sure she was deeply asleep, he laid her back in the crib and watched her for a moment, her thick, dark lashes fanning her plump baby cheeks.

'That's a beautiful lullaby.'

Larenzo stiffened, his gaze moving from his sleeping daughter to the woman standing in the doorway of the nursery. Emma's hair was tousled about her shoulders, her golden-green eyes wide and luminous. Larenzo dropped his gaze and saw with a hard kick of desire that she was wearing just what he'd imagined: a thin T-shirt that moulded to the shape of her breasts and a pair of boy shorts. He felt his body respond, and in only a pair of drawstring pyjama bottoms he knew Emma would be able to tell if she lowered her gaze just as he'd lowered his.

'She's asleep,' he whispered, and moved quietly out of the nursery, brushing past Emma as he did so. He sucked in a hard breath as her breasts nudged against his chest, and her hair whispered against his cheek. He inhaled the scent of her, sweetness and sleep, and he averted his face from the temptation of hers.

Emma closed the door behind him and they stood in the hallway, only a few inches separating them, the only light coming from a lamp Larenzo had left on in the living room, its warm glow spilling onto the floor.

It was so reminiscent of that night in the villa, the way things had shifted between them in the quiet and dark. Barriers had disappeared, defences had dropped. In that bubble of solitude and intimacy there had only been the two of them, seeking and finding both solace and pleasure.

And there were just the two of them now, standing so close together, the only sound the sigh and draw of their breathing.

'What did it mean?' Emma asked in a whisper, and Larenzo forced himself to meet her gaze, to hold himself still, when all he wanted to do was drag her into his arms, forget everything but this, *them*, for a little while.

'What did what mean?'

'The lullaby. I couldn't make out the Italian. I'm rusty, I suppose.'

'Oh… Sleep, sleep, sleep, cradle baby. Your mother is not here, she has gone away.' Belatedly he realised how it sounded. 'It's the only lullaby I know. I didn't even realise I knew it until I started singing.'

'Is it from your childhood?' Emma asked, and Larenzo blinked.

'I suppose it has to be. But I don't remember anyone singing me any lullabies.' He heard the note of bitterness that had crept into his voice and he tried to shrug it off. No point in dwelling on the past, just as he'd told Emma. 'Anyway, Ava seemed to like it.'

'Thank you,' Emma said softly, and she reached out and laid a hand on his arm. The touch of her fingers on his skin was electric, jolting his senses as if he'd stuck his finger into a socket. He held himself still, staring down at her hand, her slender fingers curled around his biceps.

She'd touched him like this back in Sicily. And he'd put his hand on hers, and for a moment he hadn't felt alone. He'd felt as if someone was on his side, someone actually cared…

But that was a lifetime ago, and it hadn't been true anyway. Their night together had been a moment out of time, out of reality. An aberration.

Larenzo forced himself to shake off her hand. 'It was nothing,' he said and without saying anything else he turned and went back to his bedroom.

Emma woke to sunlight pouring through the windows of her bedroom, and the sound of Ava gurgling with laughter from the adjoining nursery. She stretched, savouring the moment's relaxation before the day with all of its demands began.

Then she heard Larenzo's answering laughter and realised he was in the nursery with Ava. Just the rumbling sound of his voice as he talked to their daughter brought the memory of last night back with slamming force. Emma didn't think she'd seen or heard anything as beautiful, as *desirable*, as Larenzo cradling their baby to his bare chest as he sang her a lullaby in lilting Italian.

Watching him in the darkened nursery, she'd wanted him almost as much as she'd wanted him that night back at the villa. Wanted to feel his hot, hard skin against hers, his lips on hers as he treasured and cherished her with his body…

For a few seconds, when she'd touched his arm, simply because she had no longer been able to keep herself from it, she'd thought he was battling the same kind of temptation. Thought, and even hoped, that he might give in to it. In that moment she'd known if he'd kissed her she'd be lost, just as she had been before. Nothing would have kept her from him.

But he'd walked away instead, and Emma had spent a restless night trying to banish the ache of longing inside her. Now she got out of bed and hurriedly dressed in jeans and a sweater before going into the nursery.

Larenzo was dressed in an elegant and crisp suit, and he'd already changed Ava's diaper and was now wrestling her into a bodysuit. Ava was resisting him, her whole body rigid as she stared up at him in stubborn determination.

'I think she's winning,' Emma said, and Larenzo glanced up, his mouth curving wryly.

'There's no thinking about it. It's definite.'

'Do you want me to—?'

'Please.' He stepped aside and with a smile Emma finished dressing Ava, who saw that the jig was up and relaxed her body as she blew a raspberry.

'Clearly you have the touch,' Larenzo observed.

'Years, or rather, months of practice.' She turned to face

him, her heart bumping against her ribs as she realised how close he was. The woodsy scent of his aftershave tickled her nostrils and made heat lick low in her belly. 'You look smart. Are you going somewhere?'

'I have a few meetings at the office. But...' He hesitated, a note of uncertainty creeping into his voice. 'We can have breakfast first, if you'd like. I went out early this morning and bought some bagels and coffee.'

'Okay.' Emma followed him into the kitchen, Ava balanced on one hip. The smell of freshly brewed coffee and toasted bagels made her mouth water. 'So if you're not CEO of Cavelli Enterprises,' she asked, 'what are you doing exactly?'

'I'm starting a new company,' Larenzo answered as he poured them both coffees. Emma settled Ava into her high chair with a few torn-off pieces of bagel. 'LC Investments.'

'And what are you going to do?'

'I hope to invest in start-up businesses, the kind of places that might have trouble getting loans from one of the big banks.'

'That sounds rather noble.'

He shrugged and handed her a mug of steaming coffee. 'I have some sympathy for the underdog.'

Because he could relate? And yet Larenzo Cavelli was so powerful, so charismatic, so arrogant. He'd even seemed so back in Sicily when he'd been handcuffed and at the police's mercy. Standing there now, one hip braced against the counter, his large hands cradling a mug of coffee, he managed to look like the lord of all he surveyed, his confidence careless and yet utterly assured. And yet this man had come from the street.

'Did you feel like the underdog as a child?' she asked after a moment.

Larenzo pursed his lips as he considered. 'I suppose

I would have, if I'd thought about it. I was just trying to survive.'

'I'm amazed at how far you've come. You should be incredibly proud of yourself, Larenzo, going from street orphan to CEO.'

His mouth tightened and he shook his head. 'I had some help.'

Who from? she wanted to ask but decided not to. 'Even so.'

Larenzo put his empty coffee mug on the dish drainer. 'I should go,' he said shortly, and Emma felt his emotional withdrawal like a palpable thing. 'I don't know when I'll be home,' he added. 'Don't wait for me.'

Emma nodded, feeling the rejection even though she knew she shouldn't, and Larenzo left. He kissed the top of Ava's head before he went, and Emma sat down at the table to finish her coffee, caught between missing Larenzo and enjoying the prospect of a day spent in the city. She was looking forward to going out and exploring New York, and yet, even though he'd just gone, she already missed Larenzo. She was so curious about him—this man who was hardened and suspicious, who could be so ruthless and cold, and yet also showed such gentleness and kindness.

Her cell phone rang and Emma slipped it out of the pocket of her jeans, and saw that it was Meghan.

'Hey,' she said as she answered the call and Meghan drew her breath in sharply.

'Are you okay?'

'Am I okay? Yes.' Emma gazed out of the window at the view of Central Park, and then glanced at the remains of her perfectly toasted bagel. 'I'm fine. Just finishing breakfast.'

'Cavelli isn't…he's being decent to you?' Meghan asked cautiously.

'More than decent. He already has a bond with Ava. He

even got up with her in the night.' Emma pictured Larenzo wearing nothing but his pyjama bottoms, the lamplight washing over his bronzed skin, and she suppressed a shiver of desire.

'Really,' Meghan answered, the disbelief audible in her voice.

'Yes, really. I told you before, Meghan, Larenzo wants to be a part of his daughter's life.'

'I didn't realise you'd become his champion,' Meghan retorted, and Emma sucked in a breath.

'Meghan…'

'Seriously, Emma, you've changed your tune since yesterday.'

'I haven't—'

'How do you know Cavelli isn't just pretending he's interested in Ava—?'

Emma recoiled at the suggestion. 'He's not. Anyway, why would he?'

'I don't know, maybe he's trying to polish his image for the public? Whatever it is, I don't trust him, Emma, and you shouldn't either. I know the charges against him were dropped, but you know the saying, where there's smoke, there's fire.'

'And sometimes there's just smoke.' The fierceness of her response surprised them both. 'In any case,' Emma continued, 'you know as well as I do that I can't keep Larenzo from seeing his daughter.' And she didn't even want to any more. Not when she'd seen how tender he was with her.

'You still don't have to live with him. I talked to that lawyer again and mentioned that Cavelli had practically blackmailed you into living with him. It could provide evidence that he's unfit—'

'Meghan.' Shock as well as anger blazed through her. 'You have no right to talk about my business with a lawyer.'

'I'm looking out for you,' Meghan cried. 'Emma, obviously you still have some feelings for this man. That's understandable, considering your shared history. But I think you're in over your head. You don't know Cavelli, or what he's capable of. And someone has to be responsible and think about Ava—'

'I am thinking about Ava,' Emma shot back. Her voice shook with the force of her feelings. 'Trust me, I am. And Larenzo is very good with her. I don't want to keep him from Ava's life, no matter what happened in his past.'

'And what if it turns out he really is dangerous?'

'It won't. I trust Larenzo in that.'

'How can you trust—?'

'I just do, Meghan,' Emma cut her off, knowing she meant it. 'And I need to go now. Ava's starting to fuss.'

Ava, who was happily chewing on a bagel, looked at her curiously. Emma disconnected the call and flung the phone onto the kitchen counter. Her whole body was trembling.

She wanted to deny everything her sister had said; she wanted to scrub her brain and pretend she'd never heard it. And yet beneath Meghan's older-sister I-know-best attitude, Emma knew there was concern and perhaps even truth.

She still didn't know Larenzo at all. It just felt as if she did.

Ava threw the bagel onto the floor, and Emma decided it was time to go out for the day. All of New York was waiting for her to explore, and she could certainly use the distraction.

She fetched Ava's coat and hat and then buckled her into the stroller, armed with an arsenal of snacks and toys to keep her daughter entertained. Then she hit the streets.

Central Park on a crisp autumn day was one of the loveliest places on earth, Emma decided as she wheeled Ava along the twisting, tree-shaded pathways. She could hear the distant laughter of children on a playground, and some tourists were posing for photographs in front of the statue of Christopher Columbus. Every colour seemed sharp and bright, as if the whole world had been brought into crystalline focus.

As Emma strolled along Ava watched everything avidly; they made it all the way to the Central Park Zoo where they both watched the animal statues dance around the iconic clock. Emma bought a hot dog from a cart and shared it with Ava, enjoying people watching from a park bench, and then when her daughter fell asleep in her stroller she walked back uptown, stopping in front of the gorgeous esplanade with Bethesda Fountain as its magnificent centrepiece.

Every step she took felt as if she were breathing life back into her soul. She hadn't realised until then just how much of a rut she'd been in, living with her sister and staggering through her days. It had taken Larenzo's suggestion to get her out of it, and for that she was grateful.

Ava was starting to stir, and so Emma walked back towards the apartment on Central Park West. She stopped at the playground directly opposite the park's entrance and unbuckled Ava from her stroller before putting her into one of the baby swings. Ava chortled with glee as Emma pushed her, enjoying the autumn sunshine on her face.

She didn't know how long she spent in the playground with Ava, savouring the day, but it must have been more time than she'd thought for the sun was starting to sink behind the buildings on Central Park West when a hand suddenly clamped down hard on her shoulder.

Emma whirled around, her heart seeming to leap right into her throat, and saw Larenzo glaring at her ferociously.

'*Where* have you been?'

CHAPTER TEN

'YOU SCARED ME, LARENZO.' Emma shrugged off his hand and pressed her palm to her thudding heart. 'Good grief. Why did you sneak up on me like that?'

'Answer the question, Emma.'

She blinked up at him, amazed at how different he seemed now, scowling down at her, everything about him hard and fierce and utterly unyielding. Right now she could almost believe he really was a Mafioso.

'Where have I been?' she retorted, her voice rising in both anger and fear. 'Here, in the park, with Ava. It's a beautiful day and I wanted to get out and see the city.'

'You didn't tell me you were going to the park.'

'I wasn't aware I had to inform you of all of my movements.' She glared at him, conscious that the parents and caregivers around them were obviously pretending not to listen while eating up every word. 'What's with the third degree?' she demanded as she lifted Ava from the baby swing.

Larenzo was silent for a moment, the ravages of his anger still visible on his face. 'I don't like not knowing where you are.'

Emma stared at him, exasperated. 'So what are you going to do? Implant a chip in my shoulder, or how about an ankle tag? Seriously, Larenzo, I need my freedom.'

Larenzo didn't answer and with a sigh she buckled a

protesting Ava into her stroller. 'Let's go back to the apartment. We're causing a scene.'

Larenzo glanced around the playground, his scowl deepening as he saw several mothers whispering and shooting them speculative looks.

'Fine,' he said, and reached for the handles of the stroller. Emma walked beside him while he pushed Ava back towards the park entrance.

They had just reached the park gates when Larenzo stiffened, and then, shoving the stroller towards her, strode across the pathway.

Emma watched in stunned disbelief as Larenzo approached a man and without so much as a qualm took the expensive digital camera he was holding and began to push its buttons.

'Hey, you can't do that—' the man exclaimed.

'Do not,' Larenzo said, biting off each word and spitting it out, 'take pictures of my family.'

'So the rumours are true, you do have a child?'

Larenzo's face was thunderous as he handed the camera back to the man. 'I repeat, do not take photographs of my family.'

Without another word he turned back to Emma, standing there with her jaw hanging open slackly.

'Cavelli,' the man called, 'is it true that you planted the evidence on Raguso? People are saying—'

'Come on,' Larenzo said, and took the stroller from her. 'Let's go.' He began resolutely walking towards the park entrance, and mutely Emma followed.

She waited until they were back up in the penthouse apartment and Ava was settled with some toys on the floor of the living room before she started asking for answers.

'Larenzo, what on earth was that all about?'

'The photographer?' He shrugged out of his suit jacket,

not even looking at her as he answered. 'He was a member of the paparazzi. I should have known they would realise I was here. Until the press dies down, you shouldn't take Ava out in public.'

'So I'm a prisoner here?' she demanded, and Larenzo turned to look at her, his mouth twisting grimly.

'It doesn't look like a prison to me.'

She flushed, realising her poor choice of words. 'You know what I mean, Larenzo. I'll go crazy if I have to stay in here twenty-four seven.'

'For a few days only. These things never last long.'

Emma took a deep breath. 'Why does he think you planted the evidence on your business partner?'

Larenzo's nostrils flared and Emma could see how the skin around his mouth had turned white. He was angry, very angry, and yet when he spoke his voice was measured and controlled.

'Because he is trying to sell newspapers, and to do that he needs a story. Surely you know how these things work, Emma.'

She thought of her sister's phone call this morning. *Where there's smoke, there's fire.* 'Is there any truth to that claim, Larenzo?' she asked quietly.

He stared at her for a long, taut moment, and beneath the icy anger Emma thought she saw a flash of hurt in his eyes, quickly veiled.

'What exactly are you accusing me of, Emma?' he asked.

'I don't know.' Belatedly she realised what she'd been implying. She didn't really think Larenzo was guilty, but she still didn't understand him. 'I just wish I knew more, Larenzo. I feel like there are things you aren't telling me—'

'I told you, Raguso is guilty. There is no doubt. The evidence was there.'

'You said there was evidence against you—'

'Because it was planted!' Larenzo's voice rose in a sudden, anguished roar. 'It was planted, all right? I was framed, and I was too stupid and naive to realise it.' He let out a shuddering breath as he raked his hands through his hair. 'Satisfied?'

Emma didn't answer, and Ava looked up, her lip wobbling at the shouting and the tension she sensed crackling between the two adults. 'If you were framed,' Emma asked slowly, 'why didn't you tell me that from the beginning? There is no shame in it—'

'I feel shame,' Larenzo answered. He dropped his hands and looked away from her, his expression shuttered even as his voice thickened with emotion. 'I feel great shame.'

She blinked back tears at the raw pain she heard in his voice. 'Oh, Larenzo—'

'We will not discuss this any more.'

Emma could sense when a door was being slammed in her face. And yet she'd finally received some insight into Larenzo's experience, even if it left her with more questions than ever. 'All right, fine, we don't need to talk about that. But why were you so angry when you found me in the park? I don't need you to keep tabs on me—'

'I phoned the apartment several times and there was no answer. With Ava's nap schedule, I thought you would have been in the apartment at least for the afternoon. I was worried.'

'But you said there was no danger—'

'I was worried you'd left,' Larenzo said starkly. He stared at her, his face filled with bleak honesty. 'I thought you had taken Ava and left me.'

Emma gaped at him, amazed and humbled by the vulnerability she saw in Larenzo's eyes. 'If I was going to leave, Larenzo,' she said quietly, 'I'd have the decency to tell you first. And anyway, I just got here. I'm not going anywhere.'

He shrugged, his face hard and impassive once more. 'I know your sister doesn't want you here. You are close to her. She is probably like a mother figure to you since you are not close to your own mother. I was afraid she'd spoken to you, and you had changed your mind.'

Emma swallowed, stunned by his perception. 'She did speak to me. She called me this morning.'

Larenzo nodded. 'And did she tell you to go back?'

'No, but you're right, she's not happy I'm here.' She thought of mentioning the lawyer, and then decided against it. She didn't want to make Larenzo angry, or worse, to hurt him, with such information, and she had a feeling it would. This man who seemed so proud and arrogant and untouchable hid a surprising vulnerability.

'I can understand your sister's point of view,' he said, and Emma raised her eyebrows.

'Can you?'

'Of course. If I were your sister, I would be wary too. But I hope she will realise in time that you are in no danger. I hope you realise that too.'

'I do realise it, Larenzo.' Guilt lashed her that he would believe she still doubted him. 'I'm sorry I keep questioning you.'

'It's understandable,' Larenzo answered wearily. 'This is a difficult situation for all of us, but for you in particular.'

'Thank you for acknowledging that.'

He nodded, and Emma felt they'd come to a truce, and even an understanding. She took a deep breath and then bent to scoop up Ava, who had started to grizzle.

'I should start making dinner. I didn't realise how late it had become, when I was in the park.' Which was, she supposed, a sort of apology.

'I'll watch this one while you do it,' Larenzo said and, in a gesture that felt both bizarre and natural, Emma handed over Ava, who went willingly to her father.

* * *

Over the next few weeks Emma settled into a new routine that felt both comfortable and strange. Larenzo worked most days, and, after seeing to her housekeeping duties, Emma spent the days with Ava exploring the city. The autumn days continued crisp and clear and she enjoyed getting out and walking through the park, going to the Children's Museum, which Ava loved, and visiting the local shops. She'd even signed Ava up for a toddler gymnastics class, and she'd met a few other mothers at the local library's story hour. It might not have seemed much to most people, but she was more active and involved here than she'd been in her months at Meghan's.

She also developed a routine with Larenzo. An early riser, he usually got up with Ava while Emma had the unimagined luxury of a lie-in, and then they all had breakfast together in the sun-filled kitchen before Larenzo went to work. He came home no later than six or six-thirty each weekday night, and they had dinner together before bathing Ava and reading her stories, a precious hour spent as a family. Because they were a family, even if it was unexpected and unconventional. Sitting on the sofa, their daughter between them, trying to race through reading a board book before Ava tossed it to the floor, comprised some of the happiest moments Emma had ever known, and yet they also felt tenuous. Fragile. She wondered how long this 'sort of' family could really last.

At first, when Ava was asleep, they went their separate ways in the apartment. Larenzo would work in his study and Emma would read or watch TV in her room. Then one night, a week or so after she'd arrived, restlessness drove her out of her bedroom to the living room, where she scanned the shelves of expensive leather-bound books.

Larenzo came out of the kitchen, stopping when he saw her. 'Is everything all right?'

'Yes, basically.' Emma glanced over her shoulder, her mouth drying at the sight of Larenzo in faded jeans and a T-shirt, his feet bare, his hair rumpled. He looked jaw-droppingly gorgeous and just the sight of him made her belly swoop. She'd thought in the weeks since she'd been here she'd get used to seeing him, but nothing ever prepared her for the devastating sight of him, or her body's unstoppable reaction.

He cocked an eyebrow, waiting for more, and Emma let out a little laugh. 'I'm just kind of bored.'

'Why don't you go out, see a film?'

'By myself?'

'You once told me you liked your own company,' Larenzo reminded her.

'I know,' Emma admitted. 'I just don't feel like it tonight.' She was tired of being alone. Spending time with Larenzo had made her realise how wonderful and invigorating and fun company could be. *His* company.

'Well, then.' Larenzo shoved his hands in the pockets of his jeans and rocked on his heels. 'How about a game of chess?'

Remembrance rippled through her as she thought of the last game they'd played, that night in Sicily. The expectation and awareness that had tautened between them…

'Okay,' she said, and followed him into the sumptuous wood-panelled room. Two deep leather club chairs flanked a large window that overlooked Amsterdam Avenue, a low table with a chessboard between them.

Emma sat down and studied the board with its ornately carved pieces. 'I think I'm about to get my butt kicked,' she said wryly. 'Again.'

'Don't give up before you've even started,' Larenzo answered with a faint smile as he sat down opposite her. 'White moves first, remember.'

'I remember.' Those two words seemed to fall into the

stillness of the room like pebbles tossed into a well, creating ripples of awareness. Larenzo's gaze was heavy-lidded and intent as he looked at her, and Emma's heart started to thud.

'I remember too,' he said softly, and she knew he wasn't talking about chess.

She stared down at the board, the pieces blurring before her eyes as she swallowed hard. 'Do you think about it?' she asked softly. 'That night?'

Larenzo didn't answer for a long moment and she didn't dare look at him. 'All the time,' he finally said, and Emma jerked her gaze up towards his, startled and yet suddenly, blazingly hopeful. 'You should move,' he said gruffly, and, barely aware of what she was doing, she moved her knight.

They played in silence, expectation and memory uncoiling inside her, seeming to fill the room with a palpable force. It would be so easy for Larenzo to reach across the board, frame her face in his hands as he had on that night. Slide his lips across hers as she opened and yielded beneath him…

Her hand trembled and she knocked a few pieces over, scattering them across the board. 'Oh, I'm sorry,' she said, biting her lips, and Larenzo righted them easily.

'It's all right. I was going to checkmate you in three moves anyway.'

'Oh, dear.'

'Good game.' He held out his hand, his eyes glinting with both challenge and desire, and Emma took it, her fingers sliding along his as a tingle spread from her fingers all the way up her arm. His hand was so warm and dry and strong. She pulled away reluctantly.

'Another?' Larenzo suggested, and she nodded, not wanting this evening to end.

'Okay.' She moved a pawn and Larenzo countered by moving one of his. Just a few moves later Emma was down a bishop. 'I'm hopeless at this,' she said as she studied the board. Even though she was losing, she was savouring this time with Larenzo. His study was cosy and warm, the lamplight spilling across the board, the heavy damask drapes now drawn across the window.

And as for the man himself… She didn't think she'd been imagining the heat in his eyes. She certainly felt an answering desire in herself. Every so often she sneaked a glance at Larenzo's face; his eyes were narrowed as he studied the board, his mobile mouth pursed. He rested his chin in one hand and Emma longed to reach out and touch him. *Kiss him.*

She forced her gaze back to the board. 'So how did you learn chess, anyway?' she asked. 'I don't imagine they taught that at the orphanage.'

There was a slight pause and then Larenzo answered, 'My business partner taught me.'

Emma looked at him in surprise. 'Your business partner? You mean Bertrano Raguso?' Larenzo gave a short nod.

'So you really were close to him,' she said slowly.

'We were friends,' Larenzo allowed. 'Good friends.'

'Was he the one who planted the evidence against you?'

Larenzo nodded again, and realisation swooped through her. No wonder Larenzo didn't trust anyone. 'I'm sorry,' she said quietly. 'That must have been very hard, to be betrayed by someone you cared about.'

'I wondered how he could do it,' Larenzo said after a moment, his gaze on the board. 'If he was just desperate… I wish he'd told me how things were. I would have helped him.' And then, as if he felt he'd said too much, he moved his queen and put Emma into check.

The weeks slipped by and the leaves fell from the trees, creating a carpet of red and gold on the lawns and pathways of Central Park. Ava had begun to cruise, clinging to coffee tables and chair legs as she made her way around the apartment. Each Saturday Emma took her to New Jersey to visit Meghan and her family; her sister had thankfully stopped warning her about Larenzo. Meghan didn't mention him at all, which Emma supposed was better than her running him down, but she wished Meghan could see, as she now did, how different Larenzo was from what they'd both once thought.

The more time she spent with him, the more she liked him. He could be dryly amusing or gently intent, and his tenderness with Ava had brought the sting of tears to her eyes more than once. And she was having more and more trouble ignoring the chemistry between them. Just brushing past him in the elevator or touching his hand when he handed her something made Emma's insides go liquid with longing. And knowing that he remembered their night, that he might feel even just a little of what she felt...

It was the sweetest form of torture. Emma knew she had to resolve it one way or another. Either she had to stop dreaming about Larenzo, or she needed to ask him if he wanted their friendship—because she did believe they were now friends—to turn into something more. But *something* had to give, because the truth was, she acknowledged one night as she stared up at the ceiling, that she was falling in love with the father of her child.

CHAPTER ELEVEN

'WHAT'S WRONG?' LARENZO glanced up from his tablet where he'd been scanning news headlines, and Emma jumped guiltily.

'Nothing's wrong,' she said quickly, and swiped at a few crumbs on the kitchen table with a damp cloth. Ava banged her spoon on the table and then happily flung it to the floor.

Larenzo picked it up and handed it back to his daughter. 'I can tell something's bothering you,' he said mildly. 'Why don't you tell me what it is?' He tried to ignore the tightening of suspicion and fear in his gut. These last few weeks with Emma and Ava had been nearly perfect. Perhaps too perfect, because perfection wasn't real, couldn't last.

And yet he'd enjoyed this time with Emma and Ava so much…the mornings alone with Ava, and then breakfast, the three of them around the table, a *family*. He, a street rat from the slums of Palermo, finally had his own family. It felt like a miracle. It *was* a miracle. And just seeing Emma frown, sensing her disquiet, made him fear the worst now.

This family, after all, still was more façade than anything else. It wasn't as if they actually cared about each other.

Although he knew in his gut—and his heart—that that wasn't true. He cared about Ava…and he cared about Emma.

'It's nothing,' Emma said as she swiped some more

toast crumbs into her hand and deposited them into the bin. 'Really, it's nothing.'

Larenzo let it go, because he wanted to keep things the way they were, and he was worried, judging from Emma's frown, that they were already changing.

'What are you up to today?' he asked instead and she rose from the table, moving around the kitchen a bit too briskly, not meeting his eye.

'Tumbling class for Ava and then a few errands.' She gave him a brief, distracted smile. 'Nothing too exciting.'

Did he detect a note of restlessness in her voice? Was she unhappy with her life here? He knew she hadn't wanted to come here originally, but he thought in the last few weeks she'd come around. He'd believed they'd enjoyed each other's company.

But maybe he was wrong.

'Sounds fun to me,' he said lightly, and Emma just shrugged. The fear and suspicion inside him felt like acid corroding his gut. She was hiding something from him, he was sure. He knew the signs. He'd lived them.

He rose from the table and pressed a kiss to Ava's head. It took all his self-control to smile at Emma as if nothing were wrong before heading to the office.

He had rented an office in midtown to serve as the headquarters of his new operation, LC Investments. It was, Larenzo realised with every day he spent trying to set things up, going to be a long, hard slog. Even though the charges against him had been cleared, mud stuck. People assumed he had some connection to or knowledge of the criminal activity Bertrano had been neck-deep in, and he could hardly blame them. He'd been so blind. Wilfully, stupidly blind, and he would pay the price for that for the rest of his life.

All he could do now was conduct himself honourably and prove to everyone, eventually, that he was indeed an honest man.

Prove it to Emma.

Did she believe in his innocence? Sometimes, when they spent time together, when she'd gazed at him so hungrily from across the chessboard and he'd imagined hauling her into his arms…then he thought she did. But other times he remembered how she'd flung so many accusations at him, how she'd tried to hide Ava from him, and he doubted. He feared. And fear, he'd learned, was a cripplingly powerful force.

Now he pushed those churning emotions aside and focused on work. He had a meeting that afternoon with a brilliant scientist who needed funding for a new voice-recognition technology he'd patented. Larenzo was looking forward to it; it was exactly the kind of thing he'd wanted to support when he set up his new business. It was the kind of thing he'd tried to support as CEO of Cavelli Enterprises, and he'd left the running of the company's other interests to Bertrano. He wouldn't make that kind of mistake again. He knew better now than to trust anyone, not even the people you loved.

As soon as Larenzo left the apartment, Emma breathed out a discontented sigh. He was amazingly attuned to her moods, but the last thing she wanted to do was tell him what was bothering her.

Last Saturday she'd taken Ava to New Jersey to see Meghan, and the conversation she'd had with her sister had kept her up for most of the night. It had started innocuously enough, with Meghan asking her to come for Thanksgiving, which was next week.

'I'm sure we'd love to,' Emma had said. 'I'll ask Larenzo.'

'Do you need his permission to come here now?' Meghan had asked frostily, and Emma had stared at her in dismay. Over the last few weeks they'd mutually, silently agreed on a ceasefire when it came to Larenzo, but her sister had looked as if she was about to come out with guns blazing.

'No, I don't need permission,' she'd answered, although that wasn't quite true. She always asked Larenzo if she could visit her sister on the weekends, since she knew she was taking away precious time he had with Ava. Larenzo had always said yes. But she hadn't been asking for permission. Not exactly. 'I just want to make sure he's free,' she'd told Meghan, who had stared at her as if she'd sprouted a second head.

'Who cares if he's free?' Emma had stared at her in confusion and Meghan had shaken her head slowly. 'Emma, you don't actually think I'm inviting him, do you?'

'I…' She'd stopped, because of course she had thought that. It was Thanksgiving, the holiday that was meant, more than any other, to spend time with your family. And Larenzo was part of her family, whether Meghan liked it or not. 'I suppose I did,' she'd said slowly, and Meghan had shaken her head again, the movement definitive.

'Emma, let me make this clear. I will never invite that man to my house, to my family, or into my life. The fact that you even thought for a second that I would shows me just how much he has brainwashed you—'

'Give me some credit, Meghan,' Emma had snapped. 'I can judge a person for myself.'

Meghan had pressed her lips together. 'I don't think you're seeing this particular person clearly.'

'And I don't think you are,' Emma had countered. 'Meghan, everything you know about Larenzo has come from newspapers trying to sensationalise a story in order to sell more papers.'

'Do you really think he can be entirely innocent?' Meghan had asked disbelievingly. 'There was so much evidence—'

'He was framed,' Emma had answered. 'He told me so himself.'

Meghan had rolled her eyes. 'Of course he would say that.'

'I believe him.'

'Of course you do. Emma, this man could be manipulating you—'

'And if he isn't? If he's completely innocent, and you're judging him without even bothering to get to know him?' Meghan hadn't answered and Emma had pressed her point. 'Meghan, Larenzo is part of my life now. He's Ava's father, and he's a *good* father. If you continue to blackball him like this, it will only end up driving us apart.'

Meghan had paled. 'So it's him or me?' she had asked, her voice choking.

'*No.* I don't want it to be that at all.' Emma had felt near tears as she'd stared at her sister, horrified at how quickly things had escalated. 'Please, Meghan.'

'You have to make your choice,' Meghan had insisted, and Emma had stared at her helplessly.

Now, as Emma buckled Ava into her stroller to take her to her gymnastics class, she wondered just how she could make such a terrible choice. With her father in Budapest and her mother out of her life, Meghan was the only family she had, the person she'd been closest to for her entire life. The thought of losing her made everything in her cry out in despairing protest.

And yet what was Meghan really asking her? To walk away from Larenzo? Her sister knew she couldn't, not even if she wanted to, and she *didn't* want to.

Which led her to the sinking realisation that whatever she had with Larenzo was neither real nor lasting. He'd made it abundantly clear that he wasn't interested in a relationship, had no time for either trust or love. Never mind that this attraction snapped between them, or that they'd actually enjoyed each other's company. Fundamentally

Larenzo couldn't change. He'd acknowledged that himself. He'd never changed his position on looking for a relationship, and she didn't think he ever would.

If Emma was smart, she'd do what her sister suggested and keep at least an emotional distance from Larenzo. She'd even start thinking about moving out, finding her own place, her own life. She and Larenzo could come to a custody arrangement as she'd originally suggested. That was the sensible thing to do, the only thing to do, and yet everything in Emma resisted.

Which was incredibly stupid, because she knew what it was like to care about someone more than they cared about you. To have someone walk away. Better to walk away first, to be that strong.

'So are you going to tell me what's bothering you now?' Larenzo asked that evening at dinner. His voice was mild, but she felt the steel underneath his words. He didn't like her having secrets.

Emma pushed the pasta around on her plate. 'How do you know anything's bothering me?'

'Because you're a naturally cheerful person. You have this…' Larenzo gestured with his hand '…glow about you.'

Emma looked up, her heart lightening ridiculously at his words. 'Glow?'

'You light up a room.' As if realising he'd said too much, Larenzo turned back to his meal. 'So I can tell when you're not yourself.' He paused, taking a sip of wine. 'You weren't yourself when I first came to your sister's house, but I think in the weeks since then you've gained some of your glow back. For lack of a better word.' He looked up with a faint smile, although his eyes were still shadowed.

'Moving to New York was good for me,' Emma admitted.

'Despite your initial reserve,' Larenzo stated dryly.

'Don't rub it in.' She toyed with her pasta some more, choosing her words with care. 'I do want to thank you, Larenzo, for giving me this opportunity. I was stuck in a rut living at Meghan's, and I didn't even realise how deep it had become until I left.'

He nodded, and Emma knew now would be the perfect time to tell him she was ready to move on to the next phase of her life, and find her own place. A real job. The words didn't come.

'Emma?' he prompted, because he could clearly see there was more she wanted to say. *Needed* to say.

'I spoke with my sister when I visited her,' she finally said. 'She's…not pleased about me being here.'

'I knew that.'

'I mean, really not pleased. She feels I'm becoming…' She hesitated, not wanting to reveal what she was starting to feel for Larenzo yet needing to tell him something of what was going on both with Meghan and in her own heart. 'Too friendly with you,' she finally said.

'A certain amount of friendliness between us is surely beneficial to Ava,' Larenzo answered coolly. Emma could already see how he was shutting down, his silvery eyes turning to blank screens, his mouth compressing. Even the temperature in the room seemed to have dropped.

'I think so,' she answered, 'but my sister doesn't.'

'So what does she want you to do?'

'Maintain a little distance, I guess,' Emma answered after a pause. 'Keep things…businesslike.' Meghan hadn't said as much, but Emma knew her sister would be pleased if she kept her arrangement with Larenzo as simply that: an arrangement.

'If that's what you prefer,' he said in a clipped voice. 'I suppose it's reasonable.'

'You do?' She struggled to keep the hurt from her voice.

Just like that, he was going to abandon their evenings playing chess, their precious time together with Ava?

'The most important thing is that we both have a strong and loving relationship to Ava,' Larenzo answered with a shrug. 'I don't suppose it matters what we do or don't feel for each other.'

'Right,' Emma answered numbly. 'Of course.'

'I have some work to do,' Larenzo said as he rose from the table. 'I'll give Ava a bath and put her to bed, and then I'll go to my study.'

Emma nodded, accepting the rebuff, and watched as Larenzo took Ava from her high chair. She felt as if she'd just ruined whatever they'd been building together, which showed, she supposed, just how fragile it really was.

She didn't see Larenzo again that night, and the next morning he left for the office as soon as she'd come into the kitchen for breakfast. As soon as he'd gone Emma sank into a chair, Ava on her lap, and indulged in a few minutes of wretched self-pity. Larenzo had completely withdrawn from her, and she knew now she'd told him about Meghan's concerns because she'd wanted him to dispel them. She'd wanted him to tell her how glad he was that they were friendly with one another, and even more than that. That he was starting to care.

But her gamble hadn't worked, because obviously Larenzo didn't feel the way she did. At all.

She straightened, forcing the sadness back, and reached for her phone to call Meghan and tell her she'd be happy to come for Thanksgiving.

That night she told Larenzo, keeping her voice as cool as his had been, that she'd be going to see her sister for the holiday weekend, leaving Wednesday and coming back on Saturday. She didn't ask if it would be all right.

His eyes narrowed as he gazed at her. 'Four days? That seems excessive.'

'Thanksgiving is an important holiday,' she answered. 'For family,' she emphasised, wanting in that moment to hurt him, but Larenzo's face remained expressionless.

'I see,' he said as he took a sip of his after-dinner coffee. 'I wouldn't know. Very well,' he finally said. 'I suppose you can go.'

Stung, Emma flung back at him, 'I wasn't asking your permission.'

'Even so, I am giving it,' Larenzo answered evenly. 'We are equal in Ava's guardianship and care, Emma.'

'Not legally—'

His eyes flashed and he put one hand flat on the table in a gesture that was controlled and yet somehow communicated a sense of great anger, only barely leashed. 'Are you threatening me?'

'No, of course not,' she backtracked, colour rising into her face. 'I only meant that we don't actually have a formal arrangement—'

'Then I will put one in place immediately. We can consult my lawyer on Monday.'

'I already consulted a lawyer,' Emma retorted before she could think better of it, and Larenzo went even more still.

'Did you? How…interesting.'

She searched his face, empty of expression as it was, for some flicker of emotion, some sense that he cared at all, and found nothing. Had Meghan been right? Had he been manipulating her with those forays into friendliness? Considering how completely he'd cut her off now, it seemed all too possible.

'We leave tomorrow morning,' Emma said, and without waiting for a reply she left the room.

Thanksgiving was miserable. She tried to enter into the spirit of the holiday, making handprint turkeys with Ryan and helping Meghan with the pumpkin pie, but everything in her felt weighed down, as if she could barely put one foot in front of the other. Meghan, of course, noticed.

'You really do care about him,' she said quietly, when it was just the two of them on the night of Thanksgiving. The turkey had been eaten, the dishes washed and dried, the children put to bed. Pete was upstairs reading stories to Ryan as Emma and Meghan enjoyed a glass of wine in the playroom, curled up on opposite ends of the sofa.

'It doesn't matter,' Emma answered listlessly.

'Why not?'

'Because I told him what you'd said, more or less, and he withdrew completely. We used to spend the evenings together, eat meals as a—well, together.' She swallowed past the lump that was steadily forming in her throat. 'Now I barely see him.'

'Now, that's interesting.'

Emma looked up from her moody contemplation of her glass of wine. 'Oh? How so?'

Meghan sighed. 'It shows he has a sense of honour,' she said. 'Maybe.'

'What do you mean?'

'That he would see the importance of family to you. That he would respect someone else's wishes.' She sighed again, shaking her head. 'I don't know. Ever since I spoke to you I've been regretting what I said. Maybe I was too harsh, but I'm just so afraid for you, Emma.'

'I know.'

'But if he really was framed like you told me, and he is a good father like you said…' Meghan trailed off while Emma waited, impatience brimming.

'Then?' she finally demanded. 'Then what?'

'I don't know,' Meghan admitted. 'Only that maybe we're doing him a disservice. And if you actually think you could care for him, or have a relationship…'

'I think that isn't a possibility now,' Emma answered. 'He barely wants to talk to me.'

'Because you told him about my ultimatum, and then you basically chose me,' Meghan answered bluntly. 'I don't blame him, Emma.'

'I can't believe after all this you're taking his side!'

'I'm not. I'm just trying to see things as a rational adult rather than a panicked older sister.' Meghan smiled wryly. 'I'm still not sure of anything.'

'What am I supposed to do, then? Go and tell him I changed my mind?' *That* wouldn't go over well. 'I'm not sure he's a good bet as a relationship anyway, Meghan. He told me he wasn't interested in one when we first saw each other again, and that he doesn't trust anyone, ever. And I believe him.'

'And no wonder, if his business partner framed him.' Meghan sighed. 'I really don't know. If you guys did decide to get together, it would be a hard road ahead. And you aren't used to that.'

'What?' Emma nearly choked on her wine. 'What do you mean, I'm not used to that?'

'I mean, you haven't been in a serious relationship, with all of its ups and downs. You've never committed to anyone or anything for the long haul. I don't think you've ever stayed in the same place for more than a year or two.'

Emma couldn't deny the truth of her sister's words but she still felt stung. 'There's a reason for all that, you know.'

'I know, because of Mom and Dad's divorce.'

'Not just their divorce,' Emma half mumbled. 'Mom leaving the way she did…not having any interest in us…'

'You made it pretty clear you weren't interested in her, Emma,' Meghan answered gently.

'And why should I, when she rejected us?' Emma demanded.

'She asked you to live with her a year later, didn't she? Out in Arizona.'

'Yes, and that was a complete failure.' Emma shook her head, not wanting to dwell on a memory that still had the power to hurt her. 'Total disaster. I left after only two months.' Meghan was silent and Emma glanced at her suspiciously. 'What?'

'Nothing,' Meghan said as she uncurled herself from the sofa. 'But it's getting late and I want to kiss Ryan goodnight.' She hesitated and then said, 'If you really do think Larenzo is innocent, Emma, and you really do care for him, you're going to have to try. That's all I'm saying.'

'And just a few days ago you practically threatened to disinherit me if I was friendly with him,' Emma couldn't keep from reminding her sourly.

'I know, I'm sorry. I panicked. But he is Ava's father, and you do seem to care for him. So...'

'So,' Emma answered with a sigh. *So what?*

Meghan's words rattled around in her head for the rest of the visit. Did she want to try with a man who had already declared he had no interest in her, couldn't trust? And yet those evenings she'd spent with Larenzo, the way they'd been as a family, had been so incredibly sweet. And she knew he was still attracted to her, just as she was to him. But was that enough?

Emma knew he'd been hurt badly by his business partner, and was perhaps irrevocably damaged by his time in prison. Did she want to try?

She was no nearer an answer to that question when she headed back to New York on the train on Saturday evening, packed with people returning to the city after a long weekend away. Ava was fractious and the train was delayed, so by the time she stumbled into the apartment at nine o'clock at night she was completely exhausted. Ava had fallen asleep in the cab on the way back from the station, and so Emma put her right to bed.

The apartment was silent and dark, and after a second's hesitation Emma went into the hall, flicking on the lights as she looked for Larenzo.

She finally found him in the study, slouched in one of the club chairs, a tumbler of whisky in his hand. His shirt was unbuttoned so she could see the bronzed column of his throat, and his hair was rumpled, his jaw shadowed with stubble. He looked sexy and dangerous and yet also almost unbearably sad as he glanced up at her with pain-filled eyes.

'So,' he said, his voice slightly slurred from the whisky. 'You came back.'

CHAPTER TWELVE

LARENZO GAZED AT Emma standing in the doorway, her hair creating a golden nimbus about her lovely face, and thought he was seeing a vision. Perhaps he'd drunk more whisky than he'd realised.

'Larenzo…' she whispered and he straightened in his chair, flinging his glass onto the table where it clattered noisily.

'I didn't think you were going to return,' he said. She shook her head as she moved into the room.

'Why would you think that?'

'Why wouldn't I? You've made no secret of how you resent me forcing you to come here. And I know I did blackmail you, Emma. I know that wasn't honourable, but…' He raked a hand through his hair, realising his tongue was a little looser than he'd thought. He shrugged and reached for his whisky again. 'Even now I have no regrets. Does that make me a bad man?'

'No,' Emma said quietly. She came to sit in the chair opposite him, the chessboard they'd played so many enjoyable games on between them. 'It doesn't make you a bad man, Larenzo.'

'Are you sure about that?' he asked and took a final swallow of whisky. It burned all the way to his gut. 'Everyone in the world still seems to think I'm guilty.'

'I don't,' Emma whispered and Larenzo turned to look at her.

'Do you mean that?' he asked, and to his shame his voice choked slightly.

'Yes. I do.' She gazed at him with her lovely golden-green eyes, everything about her steady, trusting. And yet how could he possibly deserve her trust? How could he trust *her*?

'Emma…' he began, and then, because he couldn't keep himself from it, he reached out and curled his hands around her shoulders, then up so his fingers curved around the back of her skull and he cradled her face in his hands just as he had that night so long ago. Her skin was as soft and warm as he remembered, her lips just as full as he brushed his thumb across them.

Memories rushed through him, painful in their intensity, as Emma waited, her lips parted, her eyes closed.

How could he *not* kiss her?

And yet even as he bent his head, he resisted. He didn't want a fling with Emma, didn't want to hurt her, and yet he knew he wasn't capable of anything else. Even now, with everything in him aching with desire and longing, he knew that. He had no trust, no love, to give. And so he pulled away.

Emma opened her eyes and gazed at him for a long moment. Larenzo gazed back, and in the silence of their locked gazes he thought she understood. She sat back in her chair, disappointment twisting her features for a moment before she composed herself.

'So how was your weekend?' she finally asked and he managed a rusty laugh.

'Pretty awful. Yours?'

'The same.'

He nodded, not wanting to go any deeper with this conversation, knowing he wouldn't be able to handle it. 'I was thinking, I haven't seen any photographs of Ava from when she was small. You must have some.'

'Yes, I do. Would you like to see them?'

'Yes. Please.'

Emma nodded and then slipped from the room to re-trieve them. Larenzo leaned back in his chair and let out a shuddering breath, forcing back the desire that was still rampaging through his system. Nothing was going to hap-pen with Emma. He wouldn't let it.

She returned a few minutes later, a pink baby book in her hands. 'I don't have all that many,' she admitted, 'be-cause I was so sleep-deprived.'

'I suppose that's understandable,' he said, and Emma handed him the book. She settled back into her chair as he opened it and gazed in wonder at a photograph of Ava when she was first born, red-faced and wrinkly.

'She looks like a little old man.'

'Meghan told me most newborns do.'

'She also looks like she had a set of lungs on her even then.'

'That she did. She came out screaming and waving her fists.'

Larenzo smiled and turned the page. He studied each photograph in turn, transfixed by these images of his daugh-ter: first tiny and swaddled with tufts of dark hair, and then chubby-cheeked and bald when it had fallen out, and then sitting on a rug, showing two milk teeth as she grinned.

'These are wonderful,' he said and looked up at Emma. He was disconcerted to see affection suffusing her face, and now that the whisky had cleared from his brain he re-alised how much he had revealed a few moments ago. He cleared his throat and handed back the book. 'Are you still pursuing photography? Beyond pictures of Ava, I mean?'

The question jolted her out of her moment's reverie. Watch-ing Larenzo's face as he studied the pictures of their daughter had made Emma's insides twist with longing. He'd looked so loving, so *tender*. Now he was waiting for her answer and she straightened, shaking her head.

'Not really. I just didn't have the time or emotional energy for it.'

'You should start again,' Larenzo said firmly. 'You had such a gift, Emma.'

'It's nice of you to say so.'

'You don't believe me?'

She let out an uncertain laugh. 'No, I do. I think. I just...' She shrugged. 'I've let it fall by the wayside, I suppose.'

'Why do you think you stopped?'

Emma rolled her eyes. 'Because of a certain eleven-month-old, perhaps?'

Larenzo surveyed her thoughtfully, his silvery gaze seeming to see so much. 'Do you think that's really it?'

'What do you mean?' Emma demanded, but uncomfortably she heard Meghan's voice in her head. *You've never committed to anyone or anything for the long haul.* She'd loved photography, but she'd let it slide, hadn't figured out a way to pursue it with the demands of a baby. Hadn't committed to it.

'Are you afraid to exhibit them?' Larenzo asked.

Emma stiffened. 'Afraid?'

'Of trying and failing. Most people are.'

'Then most people are smart,' Emma answered before she could help herself. Larenzo arched an eyebrow, and she flushed. 'I mean, no one wants to fail.'

'If at first you don't succeed...' Larenzo quipped. Emma managed a small smile.

'In any case,' she said, trying for a brisker tone, 'I've never really been ambitious, for photography or anything else.'

'Why not?'

She shrugged, trying to put him off. These questions were too perceptive, too revealing. 'I always wanted to travel, live life on the road. A career seemed so stuffy.'

Larenzo nodded, not saying anything, and Emma wondered what he was thinking. Did he believe her? Did she even believe herself?

'Yet you gave up travel to have Ava,' he said after a moment, and Emma tensed.

'A decision I've never regretted.'

'Yet a surprising one all the same, considering your lifestyle choices previously.'

'Maybe,' Emma allowed, 'but you never know how you're going to feel until a situation arises. When I realised I was pregnant with Ava, and that she was a part of me…' Her throat thickened as she remembered the wondrous sense that here was a person to love, who would love her.

'A family,' Larenzo said softly and, blinking rapidly, Emma nodded.

'Yes. A family. Our family.'

Larenzo's eyes gleamed and for a moment they just stared at one another, overwhelmed by this simple yet incredible truth.

'Thank you, Emma,' Larenzo finally said, and although she didn't know what he was thanking her for, she still felt how it was a withdrawal. They were a family, but not the kind she wanted to be now.

A week slipped by, a week where Emma couldn't tell what was going on with her and Larenzo. They'd seemed to have come to a silent and somewhat uncomfortable truce, eating meals together, spending time with Ava. Yet the ease and enjoyment they'd had before that wretched conversation was gone, replaced with a polite and careful civility.

It made Emma ache for what they'd had, what they could have if both of them were willing to try. But she didn't even know if she had it in her to try, and Larenzo had given no indication that he wanted to start something more.

She remembered with an ache of longing that moment in the study when he'd almost kissed her, but he *hadn't* kissed her, even though her body had been sending out rocket flares of desire. There was no way Larenzo could have missed those signals. But he'd chosen to ease back, to pretend as if they hadn't been about to start something wonderful. She had to accept that.

Didn't she?

She wrestled with the question for a few days, wondering if she dared ask Larenzo if he would consider making their relationship romantic. The thought of him rejecting such an idea made everything in her cringe. She knew what rejection felt like. She'd kept herself from it for a reason.

Needing a distraction from her endlessly circling thoughts, she got out her camera and, with Ava in the stroller, headed for Central Park.

It was early December and the leaves had fallen, leaving the trees in the park bare, their stark branches silhouetted against a bright blue sky. Emma took a few photographs: the Bethesda fountain with its basin covered in a thin, glassy film of ice; the Mall, its cobblestones glittering with frost, the park benches that lined either side all empty; a rowboat that had come loose from its moorings and now drifted, empty, in the middle of the lake, bumping against the chunks of ice.

When Ava started grizzling from the cold, Emma headed back to the apartment. To her surprise Larenzo was home even though it was only a little after five. The sun was already starting to set, sending long, golden rays across the living room floor.

Emma unbuckled Ava from her stroller and peeled off

her puffy snowsuit; her daughter immediately started toddling towards Larenzo, her arms outstretched.

'I didn't think you'd be back yet,' Emma said. 'I haven't started dinner.'

'It's fine.' Larenzo scooped Ava up into his arms and nuzzled his face against her hair. Emma watched, a tightness growing in her chest. Would she ever get used to these unguarded moments when she saw so clearly how Larenzo loved his daughter? When his tenderness made her melt inside, and long for something she didn't think Larenzo had it in him to give her?

'I came home early because I wanted to talk to you,' Larenzo said, and he sounded so serious that Emma's heart seemed to flip right over. She didn't know whether to be excited or afraid.

As Larenzo put Ava back down and swivelled to her with an intent, sombre gaze she decided to be afraid.

'Is…is everything okay?'

'What?' He looked surprised, and his expression cleared a bit. 'Yes. Fine. Everything is fine.'

'It's just you were looking so serious.'

'No, no.' He ran a hand through his hair, rumpling it as he always did, his gaze distracted now. 'No, nothing's wrong. It's only there is a party I have to go to tomorrow night, an opening gala for a research company that is pioneering a new technology. A lot of people will be there, people I need to meet.'

'Okay,' Emma said after a brief pause. 'I suppose I can manage on my own for a night.' She'd meant it as a joke but Larenzo didn't even crack a smile. He looked even more serious than before.

'The thing is,' he said, 'I wondered if you would be willing to go with me.'

Emma's jaw nearly dropped. 'Go with you?'

'I can hire a babysitter, someone who is more than competent, and we don't have to leave until Ava is asleep.'

'Why do you want me to go with you?' Emma asked, and then could have kicked herself. Was she *trying* to get him to rescind the invitation?

He hesitated and then answered, 'I think it would be better if I bring someone to events such as this one.'

'Better? How?'

He sighed and raked his hand through his hair again. 'After everything that has happened, people still wonder if I was involved in criminal activity. I'm trying to build people's confidence and trust, and I think attending an event with you, the mother of my child, would help with that.'

Emma blinked, stung more than she wanted to reveal to Larenzo, or even to admit to herself. 'Well, at least you're being honest,' she said tartly.

Larenzo stared at her, a frown furrowing his forehead. 'You're angry.'

'Why should I be angry?' Emma countered, even though she didn't actually want Larenzo to answer that question. She was angry because for a moment her hopes had sailed sky-high as she'd thought Larenzo was actually asking her out on a date. She'd believed he wanted to be with her. But no, he was just using her as a way to restore his image, just as Meghan had once suggested. The realisation was bitter.

'I don't know why you should be angry,' Larenzo answered in that toneless voice Emma knew he used to mask his annoyance. 'I'm asking you to go to a party, that's all.'

That's all. 'Thanks for clearing that up,' she retorted and Larenzo spread his hands, clearly bewildered.

'What is wrong, Emma?'

'Nothing,' she replied, and blew out a breath. She was being unreasonable, she knew, by acting offended by Larenzo's invitation. He didn't know how she felt, how she wanted him to feel. 'Nothing,' she repeated, and lifted her camera from where it had been hanging around her neck.

Larenzo noticed, his eyes narrowing. 'Were you taking photos today?'

'I thought I might as well.'

'May I see?'

She hesitated, then, shrugging, handed him the camera. He flicked it on and began to scroll through the most recent photos, frowning slightly as he studied the images. Emma rescued Ava, who had crawled under the coffee table and managed to get herself stuck. Her heart was beating a little harder; she wanted Larenzo to like the photos. She wanted him to like *her*.

'They're good,' he said at last, 'if a bit bleak.'

A bit stung by the criticism, she grabbed the camera from him, setting Ava down with her other hand. Looking at the photos again, she realised they were rather bleak. The park had been full of people, but she'd made it look deserted. Empty and unloved. 'I suppose I was in a bit of a bleak mood,' she answered, and went in the kitchen to start dinner.

CHAPTER THIRTEEN

EMMA GAZED IN the mirror in her dressing room and felt the flutters start again in her belly. She'd spent a long time deciding on a dress; Larenzo had suggested she hit the boutiques on Fifth Avenue, the sky the limit, for her gown for the gala tonight.

While he'd watched Ava, Emma had gone out with Meghan, who had taken the train into the city, to shop. It had felt surreal and wonderfully decadent to try on designer gowns, swilling champagne and parading in front of mirrors.

'So do you think something is happening between you and Larenzo?' Meghan had asked. To her credit, her sister had been civil with Larenzo when she'd come to the apartment, and he'd been just as civil back. Still, it was a tense relationship, and perhaps it always would be.

'I don't know.' Emma had sunk onto the velvet chaise in the dressing room, the ivory satin of her gown poufing out around her. 'He told me he only was asking me because it would look good for his image.'

Meghan's mouth had curved wryly. 'At least he was honest.'

'I suppose.'

She'd gestured to the gown. 'What do you think about this one?'

Emma had glanced down at the crystal-beaded ivory

satin. 'It's gorgeous, but it looks too much like a wedding dress.'

Meghan had given her a look so full of sympathy that Emma had almost felt annoyed. She hadn't wanted to be pitied. She'd wanted to find a beautiful dress and enjoy her evening with Larenzo, no matter what his reasons for inviting her out.

Now she smoothed her hands down the bodice of the emerald satin gown she'd chosen. It was deceptively simple, strapless with a ruched bodice that clung to her figure before flaring out from her knees to her ankles. She'd left her hair loose about her shoulders and used only a little eyeliner and lip gloss to emphasise her features.

She couldn't remember the last time she'd worn something so elegant or felt so beautiful. She hoped Larenzo thought she looked beautiful. She hoped he would tell her so.

He tapped on the door of her bedroom, Ava squealing happily in his arms. 'Emma? Are you almost ready? I was just about to put Ava to bed and then we should go.'

'All right.' With one last glance at her reflection, she turned and opened the door. Her breath felt sucked right out of her lungs as she stared at Larenzo. She'd never seen him in black tie before. The crisp white tuxedo shirt emphasised his perfect physique, his chiselled jaw and bronzed skin. He held Ava, dressed in her pyjamas, balanced on one hip, and Emma didn't think she would ever see a man look so sexy and yet so heart-warmingly wonderful at the same time. Tuxedo and baby. A devastating combination.

Then she saw the blaze of heat in Larenzo's eyes and it suddenly felt hard to breathe. Hard to think. She moistened her lips with the tip of her tongue.

'Do you...do you like it?'

'The dress?' Larenzo clarified huskily. 'Yes. Yes, you look...stunning, Emma. Truly beautiful.'

'Thank you.' Her heart was beating so hard she thought he might be able to see it pounding through the fabric of her dress. She reached out to take Ava. 'I can put her to bed.'

'I don't think we should risk having her slobber on you,' Larenzo answered with a small smile. 'I'll do it. I don't mind.'

While Larenzo disappeared into the nursery with Ava, Emma fetched her matching wrap and clutch and then waited nervously in the hall. A few minutes later the baby-sitter, a competent woman in her forties whom Larenzo had hired from a well-reputed service, arrived, and then Larenzo came out, a finger to his lips.

'I think she's settled.'

He shook hands with the sitter and then, with one hand on the small of her back, he led Emma out of the apartment and into the elevator.

The elevator was huge, and yet it felt tiny and airless as they stood there, shoulders brushing, Emma's stomach clenching hard with suppressed desire.

'You look good too,' she blurted, because how could she *not* say it?

Larenzo arched an eyebrow. 'Thank you.'

She felt like an idiot, but she didn't even care. Tonight she just wanted to enjoy this time with Larenzo. Pretend, even, that it really was a date. Tomorrow they could go back to the reality of being sort of friends. Tonight was for magic.

Larenzo gazed at Emma covertly, out of the corner of his eye. She looked so very lovely standing there, like a proud, emerald flame in her dress, standing tall and straight, her chin lifted. Her hair, usually caught in a practical ponytail, was loose about her shoulders and Larenzo's palms itched with the desire and even the need to touch it. To slide his hands along her skull as he'd done the other night, but this time he wouldn't stop. He wouldn't ease away with regret. No, instead, he'd kiss her as he'd longed to then, deeply, exploring every sensitive curve and contour of her mouth, bringing her body in exquisite contact with his...

Too late Larenzo realised what this little fantasy was doing to him. He shifted discreetly, trying to ease the persistent ache in his groin, and then the doors of the elevator thankfully pinged open. It was going to be a long, uncomfortable night.

And yet he knew, as he took Emma's arm and helped her into the waiting limo, that he was going to enjoy every moment of it, with Emma by his side.

That presumption was questioned just twenty minutes later when he entered the ballroom where the gala was being held and heard the murmurs of speculation ripple through the room. Heads turned, eyes narrowed, lips pursed. Whispers seemed to mock him from every corner of the room.

Larenzo tensed, and then glanced down at Emma, who was gazing around the ballroom, enraptured. Had she noticed? Was he being too sensitive, or even paranoid? God knew he'd learned to be suspicious about everything and everyone. *Even Emma.*

Which was why they would enjoy this one evening together, and no more.

He looked up, and met the gaze of a CEO he'd been on friendly terms with before everything had come falling down. The man nodded curtly and then looked away.

In the two months since he'd been in America, Larenzo had kept a low profile, meeting privately with investors and entrepreneurs, working hard to restore his reputation one individual at a time. He hadn't gone to any major events because he hadn't wanted a reaction like this one. Yet he'd also known he needed to get out, show his face, prove to the world he had nothing to hide.

Clearly that was going to be a harder task than he'd anticipated.

Straightening, he guided Emma towards the bar in the corner. 'Champagne?' he asked and she nodded happily.

'Definitely.'

He procured glasses for them both and handed one to Emma. Tension was tightening the muscles in his shoulder blades, and he could feel the start of a headache. No one approached them, but he saw and felt the sideways glances, and knew Emma did too. She glanced up at him, her flute of champagne held to her lips.

'I see what you mean about needing to restore your image,' she said quietly.

He shrugged as if it were no matter, keeping his face blankly indifferent. He was good at that. He'd been hiding his emotions since he was a child, when the nuns at the orphanage took delight in your fear and considered any smile smug, laughter punishable.

'Shall we go chat?' Emma suggested brightly. 'That's why you're here, isn't it?'

He nodded tersely, dread pooling like acid in his stomach, corroding even the pleasure he had in being with Emma. It had been such a mistake to bring her tonight. He'd thought it would help, but now he cringed to think of her seeing his shame, the condemnation or at least awful curiosity on everyone's faces. Everyone here was wondering if he was guilty.

'Who should we talk to?' Emma pressed. 'What about the science technology guy? Is he here?'

Larenzo almost smiled at her tenacity. 'He's over there,' he said, nodding towards the other side of the ballroom, and determinedly Emma stared forward. Larenzo did smile then, wryly, and he guided her to Stephen Blane, one man, at least, who didn't think he was guilty. Or at least was willing to do business with him, guilty or not.

'Hello.' Emma stuck out her hand, which Stephen shook bemusedly. Emma was a force to be reckoned with, Larenzo thought, gazing down at her with bemused affection. She'd intimated that all of Ava's forcefulness came from him, but he knew it came from her too. She was a strong person, even if she didn't seem to realise it.

They chatted with Stephen for a while, and eventually a few other guests joined them. The conversation came in starts and stops, and Larenzo did his best to navigate its choppy waters, and ignore the occasional innuendo or sly glance, but each one rubbed him painfully raw.

Would it never end? Would he never be free from Bertrano's treachery and his own terrible mistakes?

Emma, he saw, kept her chin up the whole evening, her voice bright as she chatted determinedly with every person in their circle. But he saw the way her eyes widened when someone made some oh-so-clever quip—*How's America, Cavelli? The food's better than what you're used to, eh?*—and her body tensed. Larenzo ignored the sly innuendoes and the way people didn't always meet his eyes. They were curious, perhaps even a little afraid. He could wait it out. The people who mattered believed him.

Like Emma.

Even so, he'd never wanted her to hear this. See this. After an hour of it he'd had enough. Taking her arm, he propelled her to the dance floor.

'Let's dance.'

Clearly startled, Emma deposited her half-full flute of champagne on a waiter's tray before following him onto the floor. 'I didn't take you for a dancer.'

He wasn't, not really. 'No, why not?' he asked as he pulled her into his arms, sliding his hands down to her hips, the satin of her dress slippery under his palms. He could feel the warmth of her skin through the fabric. She draped her arms about his shoulders, her breasts brushing his chest. It was sheer torture to sway to the music and not pull her more snugly to him.

'You've always seemed so focused on work. Even when you were at the villa, you usually had your laptop with you out on the terrace. You never really relaxed, as far as I could see, except maybe a swim, and that was for exercise.'

'I know. I regret that.'

'Do you?' She tilted her head up to gaze at him, her golden-green eyes luminous, her eyebrows raised. 'Why?'

'Because I worked so hard and for what? It was all taken away in the end.' He heard bitterness spike his voice and strove to moderate his tone. 'I wish I'd enjoyed life more.'

Her lips pursed. 'You seemed to enjoy it well enough, judging from the photos I saw of you in the tabloids with one blonde beauty or another.' She glanced at him from under her lashes, waiting for his response.

His mouth tugged upwards in a smile. 'Jealous?'

'Hardly,' she scoffed.

He wished she were jealous. He wished she felt as much for him as he felt for her, even though he knew he couldn't act on it. 'That was just a form of exercise too,' he murmured, his breath fanning her cheek. He felt her shiver in response.

'Then you're obviously very fit,' she returned tartly, and he actually laughed. Emma was the only person who had ever made him laugh.

'Actually, I'm terribly out of shape. Do you know the last time I've…exercised, Emma?'

Colour washed her cheeks and he saw how her pupils dilated. This was such a dangerous conversation to have. He was flirting with fire, and yet he couldn't stop. He felt intoxicated, giddy with desire, even though he'd only had a few sips of champagne.

'I'm not sure I want to know.'

'You,' he said huskily. 'The last time was with you.'

The colour in her cheeks deepened and she looked away. Larenzo touched the tip of his finger to her chin, turned her back to face him. 'What about you?' he asked. Suddenly it was important to know.

'Me?' She let out a shaky, little laugh. 'I think the answer to that is obvious. In the nineteen months since—well, you *know*, I've been pregnant, had a baby, and been living with my sister. What do you think?'

A mixture of joy, pride, and overwhelming desire, the emotions primal and fierce, burst within him. 'Good.'

'Good?' Emma searched his face. 'Why exactly is that good, Larenzo?' she asked quietly. 'What…what are we doing here?'

He didn't answer, couldn't answer, because he knew the only thing he could say was nothing and he didn't want to say it. And Emma must have read all of that in his face for she stopped swaying to the music and broke out of his embrace.

'Excuse me,' she said, and walked quickly off the dance floor towards the ladies' room.

What was he doing? What was *she* doing? Emma stared in the mirror, saw how flushed her face was, how dark and dilated her eyes. She looked like a woman in the throes of desire. She *was* a woman in the throes of desire, and for a few exquisite moments on the dance floor she'd thought Larenzo felt something back. He'd practically been flirting with her, for heaven's sake, and then…

Then he'd pulled back. Again. Letting out a shuddering breath, Emma turned on the tap and ran cold water onto her wrists. Anything to douse this treacherous heat inside her. Every time she thought something was going to happen with Larenzo, he backed off. She didn't need to be a rocket scientist to figure out why; he'd told her himself, after all. He didn't trust people, didn't want that kind of relationship. And neither had she, for most of her life. But being with Larenzo, seeing him with Ava, had changed her.

Too bad it hadn't changed him in the same way.

Sighing, she dried her hands and turned to go back to the ballroom. Maybe she'd tell Larenzo they should call it a night. This evening had been emotionally exhausting in too many ways.

Two women brushed past Emma as they went into the ladies', their heads bent together as they gossiped. They didn't even notice her, but Emma stilled as their hushed voices penetrated the welter of her own miserable thoughts.

'He has some nerve, showing up here,' one woman said. 'I mean, *prison*.'

'It was all a bit suspect, wasn't it, his release? He confessed, after all.'

'It stinks to high heaven,' the first woman stated firmly. 'The investigation is still going on. Who knows which evidence was planted? Raguso was his mentor, you know. Like a father to him, apparently, raised him from when he was a boy. The whole thing is appalling, really.'

The women disappeared into the stalls and Emma walked out to the ballroom on stiff, wooden legs. She hadn't realised Larenzo had been *that* close to Raguso. She'd known he was his business partner, yes, but mentor? *Father figure*, raised him from when he was a boy?

And this was the man that had betrayed him?

Now his trust issues made even more terrible sense. Her steps slowed as she considered how badly Larenzo had been hurt. Could he, *would* he ever recover from that? Did she want to help him try?

You've never committed to anyone or anything for the long haul.

Could she, for Larenzo's sake? She was already falling in love with him. If she was honest, there was no falling about it. She was already there. Could she, loving him as she did, help him to heal? To trust and love again? Love *her*?

Her heart flip-flopped inside her chest like a landed fish and she pressed one hand to it as excitement and fear raced through her. She wanted to do this. She needed to try.

'You were gone a long time.'

Emma nearly jumped as Larenzo seemed to materialise next to her. She hadn't seen him approach, thanks to her whirling thoughts. Now she blinked back all the questions and offered him a smile. 'Not a very gentlemanly comment to make,' she teased, and Larenzo looked startled for a moment by her levity before he smiled faintly.

'I apologise.'

Belatedly Emma remembered how she'd left him on the dance floor. She linked her arm with his. 'Shall we dance again?'

Larenzo gazed down at her, studying her face, trying to gauge her mood.

'Please, Larenzo,' Emma said softly, and wordlessly he took her back out onto the floor.

This time when he took her in his arms Emma didn't hold anything back. She pressed her body against his, felt him tense as she wound her arms around his neck, trying to communicate in every way that she was his, that he could trust her. She knew she could hardly convince him with one dance, but it was a beginning.

It was the beginning, she hoped, of everything.

CHAPTER FOURTEEN

THEY STAYED ON the dance floor for nearly an hour, swaying to the music, needing no words. After the first dance Larenzo's body relaxed into hers, and he bowed his head so his lips brushed her hair. Emma closed her eyes and felt almost perfectly content, even as she ached for so much more. For the first time she hoped she and Larenzo might actually move on from this, to something far sweeter and deeper.

It was after eleven o'clock before they finally broke apart. Larenzo's expression was both dazed and intent as he looked down at her.

Then without any words he took her by the hand and led her off the dance floor, and away from the hotel. The December night air was a cold slap of reality but before Emma could consider what was happening between them their limo sidled to the kerb and the driver jumped out to open the door. Emma slid inside, followed by Larenzo. Their thighs touched and their hands were still linked. Neither of them spoke.

Expectation coiled more tightly inside her with every passing moment; the air felt electric, snapping with tension. Larenzo was staring straight ahead; in the darkness Emma could not see his expression, and she doubted she'd be able to read it anyway. But she *felt* his desire. She certainly felt her own.

Ten minutes passed in exquisite tension. The limo pulled up to their building and the driver opened the door.

'Good evening, Mr Cavelli,' the doorman called, but Larenzo brushed past him with no more than a nod, his hand still holding Emma's.

The elevator felt even smaller and more airless than before as they rode in silence to the penthouse. Emma could feel the heavy thuds of her heart, and each desperate breath she took sounded loud and laboured in the confines of the elevator. Larenzo's jaw was bunched, his gaze on the floor numbers as they slid past and the elevator rose higher, higher. Another breath. Her hands clenched into fists at her sides, and her wrap slithered off her shoulders, trailing to the floor.

Only a few more seconds and they would be in the apartment, they would be alone…

The doors swooshed open and Larenzo stepped out into the hallway, swiping his key card before the door creaked open. Emma followed behind him, the blood beginning to roar in her ears. She closed the door behind her as Larenzo turned to her, and even in the dim lighting of the hall she could see the hunger on his face, and it thrilled her.

He pressed her back against the door, his breathing ragged as he curled one hand around the nape of her neck and brought his lips down hard on hers.

'Mr Cavelli?'

The sound of the babysitter's voice, and her light footsteps coming down the hall, was like a bucket of ice water thrown over them. Larenzo jerked back and then turned to face the babysitter. Emma sagged against the door, disappointment swamping her along with the still-potent desire. Her lips burned.

Distantly she heard Larenzo speak to the woman, and numbly, with a murmured thanks, Emma moved aside so she could leave. The click of the door and the distant ping of the elevator seemed to echo through the foyer; Larenzo switched on the lights, bathing them both in an electric glow. Emma blinked under the bright glare, painfully conscious now at how completely the mood had been broken.

'Well.' Larenzo hesitated, his hands in the pockets of his trousers, his face partially averted from hers. 'It's late.'

Emma swallowed. 'Yes.'

The silence stretched on, but it didn't feel expectant. It felt like disappointment. Failure.

Larenzo let out a sigh so small and sad Emma almost didn't hear it. Almost didn't see the way his shoulders slumped for a single second before he straightened and turned away from her.

'Goodnight, Emma,' he said, and she watched him walk away. The click of his bedroom door shutting was as final a sound as she'd ever heard.

She stood in the hallway for a moment, then switched off the lights and breathed in the darkness. Once again Larenzo had backed off. Once again she was alone, aching with emptiness and unfulfilled desire.

But it didn't have to be this way.

The thought alone sent anticipation as well as fear racing through her, tingling every nerve ending. Quietly Emma moved through the apartment, switching on the dishwasher, tidying up the kitchen, checking on Ava. And all the while she was thinking about what she could do. What she wanted to do.

She could go in Larenzo's room, not even knock. Slip inside quietly and...

And what? Seduce him, when her only experience was that one night with him, and he had thousands of conquests notched on his proverbial bedpost?

Holding her hands up to her face, Emma let out a shaky laugh. The truth was, she had no idea what she was doing. No experience.

But she could try. Even when it was risky. Especially when it was risky. She knew bone-deep that Larenzo would keep backing off, because of his history. She was the one who needed to make the first move, take the first step. Risk her heart.

Alone in her bedroom, she gazed out at Central Park now shrouded in darkness. Her heart was starting to beat hard again, just as it had been when they'd been waiting in the elevator. When she'd been so sure something was going to happen.

But something could happen now.

Emma closed her eyes. What was the worst that Larenzo could do? Refuse her, send her back to her bedroom? It would hurt, yes, and it would be terribly awkward tomorrow, but the alternative, of doing nothing, was far worse.

Wasn't it?

Quickly she stripped off her gown and slipped on a white silk nightie that was the sexiest thing she owned. Not exactly the outfit of a great seductress, she acknowledged wryly as she glanced in the mirror. The nightie was simple but hopefully it would make her intentions clear.

Taking a deep breath, and before she could think better of it, she slipped out of her bedroom, tiptoed across the hallway, and knocked softly on Larenzo's door.

She didn't wait for him to answer, just opened the door and slipped inside, her heart beating so hard and fast she could feel it in her throat. Larenzo's bedroom was lost in shadow, the bed no more than a dark expanse in the middle, and for a moment she couldn't see Larenzo.

Then she heard his rapidly indrawn breath and she saw him standing by the window, the studs of his tuxedo shirt unfastened so it hung open, revealing the beautiful, bronzed expanse of his chest.

Emma stared at him dumbly, amazed she'd got this far and yet not knowing how to take that last step. *I've come to seduce you* sounded laughable. She moistened her lips and then croaked a beginning.

'Larenzo…'

She didn't get a chance to say anything more. As if propelled by a greater force, Larenzo strode towards her, then pulled her into his arms as his mouth came down hard and hot on hers. Excitement exploded inside her as she returned the kiss, hungry, desperate, overwhelming. Larenzo was already skimming his hands under her night-gown, tossing it the floor.

Emma pulled back his shirt; the sleeves snagged on his arms and she let out a ragged laugh as she tugged it off, the studs scattering onto the floor. She smoothed her hands along the hot, satiny skin of his chest and shoulders and let out a deep sigh of satisfaction.

She'd wanted this so, so much. And Larenzo must have too, because he barely gave her a moment to revel in the feel of him before he was carrying her to the bed, depositing her on top of the slippery satin duvet before joining her there, stretching his long, hard body out on top of hers.

She reached for the button of his trousers and with a few tugs and kicks the trousers were off, followed by his boxer shorts. Now they were both naked.

Emma drew her breath in sharply as her hand closed around the thick shaft of his arousal. Larenzo sucked in a breath too, his eyes closed, and then he leaned down and kissed her again. And again. Their limbs tangled as they drank deeply of one another, bodies pressed hot and close together, and even so Emma felt as if she couldn't get close enough.

She arched upwards as Larenzo skimmed his hand down her body before finding the juncture of her thighs and when he touched her so tenderly and yet so knowingly, she nearly wept. She'd missed this. Missed *him*, so much.

'Do you…do you have a condom?' she whispered, not wanting to break the moment but knowing she had to.

Larenzo let out a soft huff of laughter as he rolled off her. 'Actually, yes.'

Emma propped herself on her elbows. 'So you *were* hoping to get lucky,' she dared to tease.

'I guess I was. I just didn't want to admit it, even to myself.'

Her face softened and her heart ached with love for this man. This man who was such an astounding combination of pride and humility, hard and soft, need and arrogance.

'Come here,' she whispered, and held out her arms.

And Larenzo came, folding his body around her as he slid gently inside. Emma drew a quick, sharp breath at the intensity of it and he gazed down at her in concern.

'I'm not hurting you, am I?'

'No. No.' She wrapped her legs around his hips as she brought him deeper into her body. 'No,' she told him. 'Never.' It felt like a promise.

Larenzo lay with his arms around Emma, his heart still thudding and his body tingling with the aftershocks of their lovemaking. She curled her body around his, one leg across his hip, and his heart swelled with emotion, with love for her. Love he hadn't expected to feel, hadn't thought he had it in him to feel. He'd been so empty, and yet Emma had made him full again.

Yet even now he wondered. Doubted. Could this really work? He wasn't even sure what this was.

Shifting so she was resting more comfortably against him, he decided to go for light. 'So did you come in here for a reason?'

She laughed softly as she smoothed one hand down his chest. '*This* reason.'

'Ah.'

'Yes. Ah.'

They lay there in silence for a moment, and then Emma

raised herself up one elbow so she could gaze down at him. Her face was flushed, her hair like a golden-brown cloud, but her eyes were serious.

'Larenzo, at the party tonight, I overheard something.'

The sleepy relaxation that had been stealing through him vanished in an instant. 'Oh?'

'Some women in the ladies'. They said…' She nibbled her lip, and, despite the tension that was now keeping his body rigid, Larenzo felt another wave of lust crash through him. He almost reached for her again, to satisfy his desire as well as to keep her from talking. He didn't know what she was going to say, but he felt sure he didn't want to hear it. He didn't want to talk about how people had gossiped, speculated, *doubted*.

'They said Bertrano Raguso was your mentor,' she said quietly. 'Like a father to you.'

He blinked, shocked, because he'd been expecting her to talk about crime and guilt, not about Bertrano. Not about *feelings*.

'Was he?' she asked, her voice wavering slightly, and Larenzo shrugged.

'I told you we were close.'

'I suppose I didn't realise you were that close.' She hesitated, and then pressed her hand to his cheek, the simple movement nearly his undoing. 'I'm so sorry,' she whispered, and the realisation that she was sorry on his account, that she was *sad* on his account, made a lump form in Larenzo's throat and for a moment he couldn't speak.

'There's nothing you need to be sorry for,' he said gruffly as he gathered her back into his arms. 'It had nothing to do with you.'

'I'm sorry someone you cared about so much betrayed you so terribly. I thought it was bad enough that he was your business partner. But a man like a father—'

'Yes.' Larenzo stared up at the ceiling, as close to weep-ing as he'd ever been. Eventually he forced the feeling back. 'Yes, he was that.'

'How did you meet him?'

No one knew the story, and yet now, to his amazement, Larenzo realised he wanted to tell Emma. He wanted her to know.

'I was attempting to pick his pocket,' he said, and she let out a little startled laugh.

'Seriously?'

'Seriously. I was twelve. I'd been living on the streets for about a year. Surviving mainly by my wits, stealing, pickpocketing, occasionally making honest money by doing odd jobs. Sleeping rough, or sometimes in a shelter. For a few months, in winter, a couple of us clubbed together in an abandoned apartment building.'

She shivered a little in his arms. 'I can't imagine how hard that must have been.'

'It was better than the orphanage,' Larenzo answered. 'At least on the street I had control of my own destiny. In the orphanage…some of the nuns were kind. Others were needlessly cruel. They enjoyed meting out punishment, seeing our pain. I hated it.' Emma didn't answer, just put her arms more tightly around him, and absently Larenzo stroked her hand as the memories assailed him and then spilled from his lips.

'Anyway, when I was twelve, I saw Bertrano. He was in his forties then, a successful businessman. I remember his coat was the softest thing I'd ever touched. Cashmere.'

'And what happened? Did he catch you?'

'Yes, even though I must say I was a very good pick-pocket. He caught me by the scruff of my neck and shook me hard. Told me he'd take me to the police, and that I'd end up in prison if…' Larenzo broke off. He *had* ended up in prison, thanks to Bertrano. Even now it hurt.

Gently Emma stroked his cheek, brought him back from

the darkness. 'If you didn't stop?' she guessed, and he nodded.

'Yes. I ran off, didn't really think anything of it. But he found me the next day, and bought me a meal. It went on like that for a few months. I was suspicious of him, but Bertrano, I think, was lonely. He'd lost his wife and son in a car accident. He had no family.'

'And you had no family.'

'No.'

'So what happened then?' Emma asked and Larenzo forced himself to continue. The memories were harder now, tainted as they were by Bertrano's betrayal, and yet he still wanted, or at least needed, to say them.

'He offered to send me to boarding school. He wanted me to do something with myself. I didn't want to at first. I knew what institutional life was like. But then one of my friends, a boy who was only ten, died. Knifed in an alleyway, and I realised I had to get out. So I accepted, and went to a school near Rome. At first I wasn't accepted, people could tell where I came from. But I didn't care. I had warm clothes and a bed and so much food. And I actually liked the learning.'

'It must have seemed like a whole new world.'

'It did. And then I won a scholarship to university, and when I graduated Bertrano asked me to work for him.' His throat had thickened again and he stared up at the ceiling, determinedly dry-eyed. 'I joined the business, and when I was twenty-five he changed it to Raguso and Cavelli Enterprises. When I was thirty, he changed it just to Cavelli. He said he wanted to bequeath the business to me, that I'd worked hard for it, for him, and I was as good as a son.'

'He loved you,' Emma said quietly. Larenzo swallowed.

'And I loved him. Which has made it all the harder to accept how he was willing to betray me.'

They were both silent, their bodies still wrapped around

one another's, the only sound their breathing. Eventually Emma stirred a bit.

'Do you think he's regretted what he did to you?' she asked quietly.

'I don't know,' Larenzo admitted. 'Even now I want to give him the benefit of the doubt. I want to believe he was just weak and afraid. I don't think he had criminal connections the whole time. I'd left a lot of areas of the company to him, and I think he got in over his head.'

'And that's why you confessed.'

'I confessed because the proof was there. I was CEO of the company, and Bertrano had put my name all over his shady dealings. I'd put my name all over it, by giving him that leeway.'

'You still could have fought it, Larenzo,' Emma insisted. 'But you didn't because you loved him. Because you were protecting him.'

He closed his eyes against the memory, and her flawless, painful understanding. 'Yes.'

She placed one hand on his cheek, forcing him to look down at her. 'That is nothing to be ashamed of.'

'Isn't it?' he demanded rawly. 'He might have loved me as his son once, but he still treated me as his stooge. And I let him.'

'He was an old, weak, frightened man.'

'You're pardoning him?' Larenzo demanded and Emma shook her head, certainty blazing from her eyes.

'No. I'm pardoning you.'

He took her hand in his then, and pressed it to his lips. Their gazes held, the communication between them silent and pure. *You are understood. Forgiven. Loved.*

'Thank you,' he whispered and she smiled even as her eyes filled with tears.

'Do you know that's what you said after the last time we made love? You don't need to thank me, Larenzo.'

'I've never told anyone all of that before,' he said. 'I'm grateful that you listened. That you understood.'

'I'm grateful you told me,' she answered, and they didn't speak after that. They didn't need to.

CHAPTER FIFTEEN

THE NEXT MORNING Emma got up with Ava while Larenzo slept. The sleep of the just, she thought with a wry smile as she gazed down at him. He looked glorious stretched out in bed, the sheet tangled around his hips, one arm thrown over his head, the morning sunlight touching his body with gold.

Ava let out another yowl and reluctantly Emma turned away from Larenzo. Her heart was light as she changed and fed Ava; last night things had finally shifted. Larenzo's story of his childhood made her heart ache with sorrow and grief for the lonely boy he'd been, but she was also thankful, so thankful, that he'd told her. They could go on from here, Emma thought. They could build something strong and true. Last night they had laid its foundation.

She was standing by the stove, scrambling eggs, Ava sitting in her high chair banging a spoon on the tray, when Larenzo came into the kitchen. He'd changed into jeans and a T-shirt but his hair was still rumpled, his jaw dark with stubble, and he looked so sexy that Emma's insides clenched hard on a spasm of longing.

'Hey,' he said, and she just about managed to keep her voice sounding normal as she answered.

'Hey.'

'Dada!' They both looked in surprise at Ava and then at each other as she proudly said it again. 'Dada.'

'That's right, sweetheart,' Emma said, her voice a little choked, and Larenzo scooped his daughter up into his arms.

'Aren't you the clever one?'

Ava grinned and patted his cheeks and then squirmed to get down. Larenzo let her down, watching in bemusement as she cruised from chair to table leg. 'She really will be walking soon.'

'Yes, maybe by Christmas.' Which was only a few weeks away. Emma turned back to the eggs and a silence stretched between them, one that was not precisely uncomfortable, but not comfortable either. She didn't know what it was...or what was happening between them.

'Emma,' Larenzo said finally, and she braced herself against that tone.

'Don't,' she said softly, her back to him as she stared down at the mess of eggs. 'Don't try to let me down easily, Larenzo. Not after last night. Not after everything.'

She heard him sigh, a long, weary sound. 'I'm grateful for last night,' he said. 'For...for everything.'

'But?' she prompted, and heard how her voice wavered. She didn't wait for him to tell her. 'Let me guess. But you don't have anything to give because you've been too hurt. You can't trust anyone. You're not looking for a relationship. Yada-yada-yada.'

Larenzo didn't answer and Emma forced herself to turn around. She could feel the tears start in her eyes and she blinked them back, determined to be angry instead of afraid. Strong instead of weak. 'Am I right?'

'A few weeks ago,' Larenzo said slowly. 'A few days ago, even, you were right.'

The first frail thread of hope began to unspool inside her soul. 'But?' she prompted again, and this time she waited.

'But I don't want to live my life in an emotional void. Perhaps I needed that for a while, after everything. It was a way of protecting myself, I suppose. Of...healing.'

'You're a regular armadillo,' she managed to tease, and he offered the most wonderful, crooked smile.

'That's me.' He didn't say anything more and Emma drew in a deep breath.

'Larenzo, are you telling me, in your awkward, emotionally stunted way, that you actually want to try something? With me? A relationship?'

He rubbed a hand over his face. 'Yes, in my—what was it? Awkward, emotionally stunted way, I am.'

With a laugh Emma rushed into his arms. Ava, clinging to a kitchen cupboard, regarded them both curiously as Emma buried her face in Larenzo's shirt and tried not to weep. 'I'm just happy,' she said with a trembling laugh and a sniff, and Larenzo stroked her hair.

'I am too,' he said, and he sounded wondering. 'But, Emma, the other stuff still applies. I don't…I don't know how much I have in me. I still don't feel…' He paused, searching for words, and Emma waited. 'Like a whole man. As if I've truly put the past behind me.'

'You've taken steps,' Emma answered firmly. 'That's the important thing, Larenzo. You can't expect everything to fall into place all at once. But it will.' She believed that absolutely. 'It will.'

He nodded, still looking doubtful, and she continued, 'And the past will always be there. You can't forget it. You can only learn to live with it.'

'With your help,' Larenzo said, and put his arms around her. Emma couldn't remember when she'd felt so happy, so *joyful*.

'Now I know what the woman in the photo feels like,' she said and Larenzo smiled faintly before kissing her lips.

'So do I.'

They had nearly three weeks of that joy. Things went on the same in many ways; Larenzo still worked, and Emma still stayed at home with Ava. But everything felt different. Everything *was* different, because they were a family now, in every sense.

Larenzo kissed her the moment he got home from work, and Ava squealed to be picked up. They spent the evenings together, watching a DVD or playing a game or just chatting; sometimes they would sit on the sofa, Emma's feet in Larenzo's lap while he worked and she studied the photographs she'd taken that day.

Her creativity had exploded along with her joy; suddenly she saw pictures everywhere, and she spent many crisp wintry days trawling the city streets with Ava in tow, snapping photos and capturing moments. So many wonderful moments.

'You really should try to exhibit these,' Larenzo said when she showed him her latest round of photos, candids of various people around the city who had been happy to have their picture taken.

'I wouldn't even know how to begin,' Emma answered. 'But I'll think about it. I'm just happy to be feeling creative again. I felt dormant for so long, just struggling through each day.'

'I know how that feels.'

'Was that...was that how you were in prison?' she asked hesitantly. They still hadn't talked about his time in prison, and after that one night of confession they hadn't spoken about the past at all. They were, as Larenzo had said, focused on the future. Their future.

'I suppose,' he answered now. 'I felt...not just dormant, but dead inside. As if there was nothing left to live for. As if I wasn't even alive, not in the way that counted.'

'And when you realised you could walk free?' she asked softly. 'That new evidence had been found?'

'It didn't sink in for a while. I didn't believe it, at first.

And then when I actually got out…' He shook his head. 'Feelings don't go away as quickly as that. I still felt empty.'

'And now?' she whispered.

'I'm filling up,' he told her, and she laughed to see the wicked gleam enter his eyes. 'You're filling me up,' he said, and reached for her.

If the days continued on as normal, the nights were wonderfully changed, long and pleasure-filled. Emma didn't think she'd ever tire of exploring Larenzo's amazing body, or having him revere hers. She wondered how she'd lived so long without knowing the pleasure of such intimacy with another person.

Larenzo clearly wondered the same thing, for one night after they'd made love he ran his hand along her hip and asked, 'So how come you were a virgin at age what? Twenty-six?'

She wriggled around to face him. 'Is it really so odd?'

'In this day and age, I'd say so.'

She shrugged. 'I just never met the right guy, I suppose.'

'But you must have had boyfriends.'

She hesitated, uncomfortably aware at how this conversation was leading them both into the uncharted and unknown territory of her past. 'A few, but no one serious. Obviously.'

'So?'

'I didn't want to get that close to somebody,' Emma said after a moment. 'I liked being on my own.'

'Why?' Larenzo asked, frowning.

'I suppose my parents' divorce affected me badly,' Emma admitted. Larenzo had been honest with her about so much; the least she could do was be honest in return. And it was hardly as if she had some great tragedy or injustice in her past, not as he had. 'My mother left,' she continued. 'When I was twelve. She'd had enough of moving every two or three years. She wanted to return to the States, live in one place.'

'And your father didn't want to?'

'I don't know if she gave him a choice. I wasn't aware of any tension or fights, at least. Just one morning at breakfast she told us all she was leaving. Going back to America. I thought she meant for a vacation.'

'And she didn't take you?'

'No.' Emma shook her head, the memory making her eyes sting even now. 'No, she didn't even suggest it. In fact...' She trailed off, and Larenzo slid his hand in hers, a small gesture of solidarity that strengthened her to continue. 'In fact, I asked her to take me. I was closer to her than to my father, mainly because he was so wrapped up in his work. And...she said no.'

'I'm sorry, Emma,' he said quietly.

'So am I.' She sighed and rolled onto her back. 'It is a terrible feeling, to be rejected like that by your own mother.'

'Yes,' Larenzo agreed. 'It is.'

Emma stiffened. 'I'm so stupid and callous,' she exclaimed. 'I'm sorry—'

'No, don't be.' He smiled and stroked his hand back up her hip, all the way to her shoulder. 'We were talking about you. Why do you think she said no?'

'I don't know. I didn't ask. I acted kind of bratty, to be honest, and made like I wanted to be with my dad anyway. And she went off to Arizona and met someone else.' Those were the facts, and yet Emma thought Larenzo could guess at the years of confusion and pain she'd felt at the way her mother had so easily left her.

'And then what happened?' he asked.

'We lost touch over the years. She did ask me to visit, to live with her for a year, when I was in high school. I went, and it was so awkward and just...awful. She was wrapped up in this new guy and he didn't want to have anything to do with me.' She paused, remembering the tension, the arguments, the misery. 'I told her I was leaving, and she didn't even seem to care.' She remembered telling her mother she was going, willing her to insist she wanted her to stay. She hadn't. 'I suppose it felt like another kind of rejection. After that we hardly spoke or saw each other at all.'

Larenzo gathered her up in his arms. 'And that made you stay away from real relationships?'

'I guess, although I didn't connect the dots that simply. But I've always moved around a lot, and I've spent a lot of time on my own. I never felt like I needed anything or anyone else.'

'So what changed you?'

'You did,' she said simply. 'You were the first person that made me want to be different.'

'I'm glad,' Larenzo said softly. 'Because you made me want to be different too.'

And during those few weeks, their happiness was not unalloyed; the past continued to mar the perfect landscape of their joy, as Emma had known it would, as she'd warned Larenzo it would, and yet...

It was hard. Harder than she'd expected.

More than once she woke up in the middle of the night to an empty bed, and when she went in search of Larenzo she'd find him in his study, working or sometimes just staring into space.

'I've had trouble sleeping since prison,' he told her, but Emma saw the way his gaze flicked away from hers, and she felt there was more he wasn't saying.

Several times she went out with Ava and returned late, to be faced with Larenzo's sudden and inexplicable wrath.

'You should have phoned,' he stormed one night when Emma had come back after dinner.

'I tried,' she answered as calmly as she could. Ava was squirming to get out of her snowsuit. 'But the reception was bad—'

'In Manhattan?' he scoffed. 'You can get reception anywhere. Or were you not in Manhattan?'

Emma sat back on her heels and looked up, meeting his gaze steadily. 'Are you accusing me of something, Larenzo?' she asked quietly and he sagged suddenly, looking older than his thirty-five years.

'No. No, of course not,' he said, and they both dropped it, but each of those tense interactions made Emma weary. Understanding someone had trust issues and living with it were two very different things.

But even worse than Larenzo's bouts of suspicion were the dark moods that overtook him so he retreated into himself and nothing Emma did could reach him. Eventually he'd come out of it again, whether it was hours or days, and he would shoot her a look of apology that Emma accepted with a silent nod. He had hard memories; she understood that. It didn't make it any easier to deal with.

The week before Christmas she went to New Jersey with Ava to visit Meghan. She'd already told her sister she would be spending Christmas in the city with Larenzo; Meghan had been disappointed but understanding.

'You look tired,' she said when she met Emma at the train station. 'Is Ava keeping you up at night?'

'No, she's actually sleeping through for once.' Emma opened the car door and began to buckle Ava into her car seat. 'I'm fine.' She avoided her sister's gaze as she said it; the truth was, she was tired because Larenzo had been up in the night, unable to sleep, and when Emma had confronted him about it he'd become angry and stalked off. In the morning they hadn't mentioned the argument, and now Emma wondered if it would always be like this.

'Are you happy?' Meghan asked bluntly. 'With Larenzo? Because I'll be honest, Em, you don't actually look that happy.'

'I am happy,' Emma protested. 'I love him.'

'Loving someone doesn't always equal happiness.'

'It should,' Emma answered as she stared out of the window. 'It should,' she said again, and she heard the defeat in her voice.

They drove in silence for a few minutes, the muted landscape of the suburbs in winter streaming by. 'So what's going on?' Meghan asked eventually. 'Because obviously something is.'

Emma sighed. 'Nothing, really, it's just…you were right. It's hard sometimes. Larenzo has a lot of…'

'Emotional baggage?'

'Yes. But I do too,' Emma said quickly, and to her surprise Meghan nodded.

'More than you think.'

'Now what's that supposed to mean?'

'Come on, Emma. Most people whose parents divorced when they were kids manage to get over it and have healthy relationships of their own.'

Emma stiffened. 'So what are you saying exactly? That I'm some kind of freak?'

'No, of course not,' Meghan answered. 'But Mom leaving was really hard on you. Maybe because of our lifestyle growing up, all the moves, all the different cities and schools. You never had a friend for long.'

'I know.' When she'd been about eight or so she'd stopped investing so much in friendships. In the circuit of international schools, people were always on the move. And she hadn't minded; you had a friend for a while, and then someone left, and you found someone else. It had been simple—until her mother had been the one to find someone else.

'So perhaps that's why Mom leaving you affected you so much,' Meghan finished gently. Emma stared out of the window.

'I asked her to take me with her,' she said after a moment. 'I don't think you knew that.'

'No,' Meghan said quietly. 'I didn't.'

'She said no. Obviously.' Emma took a deep breath. 'So that might be the reason why I'm a little gun-shy when it comes to relationships.'

'Maybe,' Meghan allowed, and Emma could tell she wanted to say something else.

'What is it? You might as well give it to me straight. It's not like you to hold back.'

'There was…stuff Mom didn't tell you,' Meghan said slowly. 'Because you were so young.'

'Stuff?' Emma stiffened. 'What kind of stuff?'

'She was depressed,' Meghan answered after a moment. 'Really depressed. She told me about it, when I was in college. She was trying to get help, but it was hard.'

'Depressed…?'

'Did you never notice anything? How tired she was, and how…I don't know…listless sometimes?'

Distantly Emma recalled how much her mother had slept. Often when she'd come home from school, her mother would be napping. She hadn't thought much of it, perhaps because she'd had no one to compare her mother to. 'I don't know,' she said finally. 'Maybe, a bit, but…'

'When she went back to America she went into a clinic,' Meghan said. 'For depression. She was there for six months. That's why you couldn't come.'

Emma swivelled to gape at her sister. 'And she never told me? Not once, in fifteen years?'

'I think she felt ashamed,' Meghan said quietly.

Emma sank back against the seat. Just as Larenzo had felt ashamed. And yet in both cases honesty, although harder, would have been so much better. So much more healing.

'I wish I'd known,' she muttered. 'She could have told me when I came to live with her.'

'I think she just wanted to forget that part of her past, of herself.'

'And that visit was a disaster,' Emma reminded her. 'It wasn't just about the depression, Meghan.'

'I'm not saying it was. I just wanted you to understand the whole picture. As for that time in Arizona…you left pretty quickly, Emma. Maybe that felt to Mom like you were rejecting her.'

'So you're blaming me?' Emma demanded, more hurt than she wanted to admit or reveal.

'No, I'm only asking you to look at it from both sides.'

Meghan fell silent, and Emma turned back to the window. Look at it from both sides? She realised she'd been clinging to her entitlement as the wronged party for so long. Her mother had rejected her. Her mother had failed her. It was a child's view, and one she wasn't actually all that proud of.

She wanted things to be different with Larenzo. *She* wanted to be different, to be patient and understanding of the man she loved, and to trust that he would put the past to rest, stay with her and love her for ever…even if he had trouble trusting her in the same way.

'Love is complicated,' she finally said to Meghan, and her sister laughed.

'You've got that right.'

Her conversation with Meghan was still rattling around in her head when she returned to New York that evening. Meghan had helped her to deal with her past issues, and maybe she needed to help Larenzo deal with his. Not just by being patient or loving, not just by waiting, but by dealing with them once and for all.

Ava had fallen asleep on the train, and Emma hefted her over one shoulder as she wriggled her way out of the cab and then up to the apartment.

Larenzo met her at the door, taking Ava from her aching arms. He put Ava to bed and then rejoined her in the living room, looking slightly wary, as he always did after she'd returned from her sister's. As if he were still afraid she might leave him.

'Larenzo, I've realised something,' she said, and now he looked even more suspicious.

'Oh?'

'We can't go on like this.'

He stilled, his face wiped of expression. 'I see.'

'No, you don't,' she said in exasperation. 'I'm not leaving you. I want you to leave me, for a little while.' He stared at her, nonplussed, and she took a deep breath. 'I want you to go back to Sicily.'

Larenzo's eyebrows snapped together. 'No. Never.'

'I want you to see Bertrano.'

'No,' he said again, his voice as hard as she'd ever heard it. 'I have no desire to see him again, Emma. Ever.'

'Don't you think you need closure?' Emma asked softly. 'For both our sakes? Meghan was talking to me and I realised how much of my past I'd avoided. I thought I could put all my bad memories in a box and pretend they didn't exist. But it doesn't work that way.'

'It can.'

'Please, Larenzo. Just to finally learn why he did what he did. To make peace with it, if you can.'

Larenzo flicked his gaze away from hers. 'And if I can't?'

'You can, Larenzo.' Emma laid her hand on his arm. 'I know you can.'

He said nothing for a long, long moment, and she could see the emotions battling in his eyes, on his face. Then slowly, painfully, he nodded.

CHAPTER SIXTEEN

LARENZO STOOD IN the small waiting room of the high-security prison near Terni, in central Italy. Sweat prickled his scalp and his stomach did a queasy flip. Just a little over two months ago he'd been behind those locked steel doors. He'd walked out a free man, but returning to the place where he'd felt so hopeless was not a comfortable feeling.

He took a deep breath and let it out slowly. He'd been waiting for fifteen minutes for the guard to tell Bertrano he had a visitor. Larenzo hadn't asked his former mentor if he could visit; he hadn't wanted to give Bertrano the opportunity to refuse. And he hoped, now that he was actually here, Bertrano wouldn't. He'd realised, in the few days since Emma had confronted him, that she'd been right. He needed to talk to Bertrano. He needed to understand.

'Come with me,' the guard told him in Italian, and with a terse nod Larenzo followed him through the heavy steel door, past the metal detector, and then to a holding cell where he was patted down before finally emerging in the visiting room, a dour place with half a dozen non-contact phone booths. Bertrano waited in one.

Just the sight of him caused shock and something worse, something like loss, to jolt through him. Bertrano was slouched in his chair, his face haggard and lined so he looked far older than his sixty-seven years. He lifted his bleary glance to Larenzo as he sat down, then looked away again, seemingly indifferent.

Larenzo took a deep, even breath and then picked up the phone. After a moment Bertrano picked up his.

'So you came,' he said flatly.

'Yes. I came. Which is more than I can say you did for me.' He hadn't wanted to start this conversation with bitterness, yet he couldn't seem to keep himself from it. Bertrano just shrugged. 'Did you think I wouldn't?' Larenzo asked, and the old man shrugged again.

'Frankly,' he answered, 'I didn't really care.'

Larenzo blinked. He realised he'd expected Bertrano's shame, his guilt, his anger, even his defensiveness…but this indifference shocked him.

'Why?' he asked eventually.

Bertrano glanced at him, shaggy eyebrows raised. 'Why what?'

'Why did you do it?' Larenzo asked, his voice low. 'I thought about it many times. I had many hours in prison to think about why you would betray me in such a fashion.'

To his amazement Bertrano let out a hoarse, rasping laugh. 'Betray you?' he repeated. 'Even now, you can think that?'

Larenzo stared at him. 'What do you mean?'

Slowly Bertrano shook his head. 'After all this time,' he said. 'After everything I've done, you still want an explanation? Isn't it obvious, Larenzo? Or are you just being blind? *Cazzaro,*' he spat, and Larenzo recoiled at the insult.

'I am not an idiot,' he said coolly. 'I am trying to understand—'

'Understand what? It's all pretty simple to me. I used you, Larenzo. I framed you. Which part don't you understand?' He shook his head before looking away.

'I know that. What I don't understand is how you could do such a thing, after all—' he broke off, feeling a pressure building in his chest, before he continued tightly '—after all our time together. You rescued me, Bertrano.

You *saved* me, you treated me with such kindness, and then to betray—'

'Oh, enough with the hurt feelings,' Bertrano said, flapping his hand. 'Enough, enough.' He leaned forward, his eyes glittering with a malice Larenzo had never seen before. 'Why do you think I saved you, Larenzo? You, a Palermo street rat, worthless, hopeless, rough and untaught? Why would I save *you*?'

Larenzo stared at him, the pressure in his chest painful now, taking over his whole body. He stared at the man he'd once thought of as his father and could not speak.

'No answer, eh?' Bertrano nodded. 'That's because the only answer is the one you've refused to accept, even when it was staring you in the face. You were my safety net, Larenzo. My backup plan. No more than that.'

Larenzo's hand was clenched so hard around the phone his fingers ached and his knuckles were white. 'Tell me what you mean,' he demanded.

'I wanted someone I could blame,' Bertrano said simply. 'That's all you ever were. What is the English expression?' He closed his eyes briefly, his mouth curving in a cold, cruel smile. 'A stooge.'

Larenzo didn't answer, couldn't speak. The question that burned in his throat was one he was too ashamed to say. And yet somehow he found himself saying it, needed to say it. To hear the answer. 'Didn't…didn't you ever care about me?'

Bertrano gazed at him pitilessly. 'No.'

And still he resisted that awful truth. 'But so many years…my schooling, the business…' But he wasn't thinking of that. He was remembering days at the beach, and evenings playing chess, and the way he'd felt loved and accepted by Bertrano. All of it false? All of it a *ploy*? He shook his head, unable to process it. Desperate to deny it.

'I was fond of you,' Bertrano allowed, 'in a way. You

were so eager to please, after all. But the reason I sought you out, Larenzo, was so I could put the blame on you if it all went bad.' He sagged against his seat. 'Which, of course, it did.' He shook his head. 'Your lawyers were tenacious, I'll grant you that. I thought I'd destroyed any evidence that could convict me. I suppose it's my own fault.' He shrugged wearily and looked away, a man who no longer had any hope. Just as Larenzo had been. Just as he felt now, for he was starting to see how it all made terrible sense.

The questions Bertrano had first asked, about whether he had family, or if anyone would come looking for him. Anyone who would care. And then how Bertrano had encouraged Larenzo to pursue his separate business interests while he tended to the rest. Putting the business into Larenzo's name. He'd thought Bertrano was being kind, but he'd actually just been constructing an elaborate web in which to ensnare him. All of it, everything, had been false. A lie. This was so much worse than what Larenzo had thought. Grief poured through him in an unrelenting river, a grief deeper and darker than any he had known before.

Bertrano let out a weary sigh. 'Poor Larenzo,' he mocked. 'Always wanting to be loved.'

Larenzo could take no more. He slammed the phone down so hard it cracked the cradle and then walked out of the visiting room without looking back.

Outside he braced his hands against the roof of his hired car and took several deep, even breaths to calm his racing heart.

All of it a lie. All of it a ploy.

Even now, he could scarcely believe it. This was what he'd come back for? This was to help him move on? Then, with a new, cold clarity stealing over him, Larenzo realised it would. Because now he knew that nothing was real. No one could be trusted.

* * *

Emma paced the living room restlessly, trying to suppress the anxiety that had settled like a stone in her stomach, weighing her down. Larenzo had been gone three days. He was due back tomorrow, on Christmas Eve, and yet he hadn't contacted her in over forty-eight hours. The last time she'd spoken to him had been when he'd arrived in Terni, intending to visit Bertrano in the morning. He'd sounded resolute and yet also upbeat, and Emma had felt so thankful for his willingness to do this, so admiring of his courage. Now she wondered sickly just what he had found.

She tweaked an ornament on the Christmas tree she'd had the doorman bring up to the apartment. She'd bought it outside the Natural History Museum, a mammoth tree whose top touched the ceiling. Ava was enchanted by it, but it meant Emma had had to decorate only the top half of the tree so her newly walking daughter couldn't pull all the decorations off.

Still, she thought the apartment looked beautiful, decorated for Christmas. Besides the tree she'd bought a nativity scene and set it up in the hall. Boughs of evergreen and holly garlanded every doorway, and filled the rooms with their fresh, spicy scent. She glanced under the tree to where she'd put several presents: a few toys for Ava, and a photograph for Larenzo. Her chest tightened as she thought of them all spending Christmas together, a family.

Why did she feel now as if it might not happen? *Why had he not called her?*

She heard the sound of the front door opening and everything in her stilled. Larenzo wasn't due back until tomorrow and yet he was the only one with a key card. Then she heard the slow, deliberate tread, and Larenzo appeared in the doorway. He looked…he looked as he had that night so long ago now when he'd come to the villa. Haggard. Resigned. As if he was missing an elemental part of himself.

Emma pressed one hand to her hard-beating heart. 'Larenzo. I wasn't expecting you until tomorrow.'

He tossed his key card on the table and walked past her, to the drinks cabinet, just as he had before.

'I decided to come home early.'

'Why didn't you call?' Not wanting to sound accusing, Emma strove to moderate her tone. 'I was worried about you. What…what happened with Bertrano?'

Larenzo poured himself a whisky, his back to her. 'He told me the truth.'

'What do you mean—?'

'It was very enlightening,' he cut across her. He turned around, the tumbler of whisky held to his lips as he leaned against the cabinet. 'Very enlightening,' he repeated, and took a long swallow.

Emma shook her head slowly. 'Why don't you enlighten me, then?' she asked, trying to smile. 'I was worried.'

'Were you?' He sounded disbelieving and Emma's insides lurched with fear.

'Yes, I was. Please, Larenzo. Tell me what is going on.'

'Perhaps you should tell me what's going on,' Larenzo returned coolly. 'Because it occurred to me, Emma, how easily you agreed to come live with me here. For a woman who was hell-bent on keeping me from her child, you changed your tune rather quickly. Rather conveniently.' He took another sip of whisky, watching her all the while through narrowed eyes.

'I don't understand what you're implying, Larenzo,' Emma answered. She tried to keep her voice calm, although she felt like screaming. Like flying at him and slapping some sense into him, because she could see he was in self-destruct mode and she didn't know how to get him to stop. 'Larenzo, please. Let's talk about this…'

'I am talking about this. I'm talking about the fact that you were desperate to have me out of your and Ava's lives, and then all of a sudden you changed. You'd called a lawyer, after all. You were serious, Emma. And then you just caved. Why?'

'Because I realised I wanted you involved in Ava's life,' she answered steadily. 'I know what it's like to have an absentee parent and I didn't want that for Ava. I didn't want that for you. You're a good father, Larenzo.' He didn't answer and Emma took a step towards him. 'Please tell me what happened in Italy.'

'What happened is I woke up and realised how deluded I've been about people. Everyone wants something, Emma. Everyone's looking out for the main chance. Even you. Especially you.'

She gasped, the sound one of pure pain. '*Especially* me?'

'You've got a pretty sweet deal here, haven't you? Luxury apartment in the city, every expense paid for.'

'I offered to pay my way—'

'Of course you would. You'd want to seem convincing.'

'Convincing? Convincing of what?'

'You wanted me to look out for you. To take care of you. Maybe you're even hoping for marriage.'

She shook her head slowly. 'What on earth has got into you, Larenzo? What did that evil man say to you?'

'Evil man? But you said he was just weak and afraid. You had quite a lot of sympathy for him, as I recall.'

'I had sympathy for you,' she corrected. 'Although it's disappearing fast.'

'Is it?' Larenzo's mouth curved in a cold smile. 'Good.'

'Good? *Good?*' Her voice rose in a scream as her hands clenched into fists. 'Are you going to throw away everything we've built together simply because of something Bertrano said to you?'

'Everything we've built?' Larenzo arched an eyebrow. 'It doesn't seem that much to me. A few weeks, Emma. That's all.'

Emma gaped at him, unable to believe that everything could fall apart so quickly. So utterly. 'What are you saying, Larenzo?' she demanded. 'How does Ava fit into any of this?'

'Ava is my daughter and I will have a place in her life,' Larenzo answered. 'Always. That won't change.'

'But us?' Emma forced herself to ask. 'What about us?'

For a second, no more, Larenzo looked conflicted. Tormented. Then his expression ironed out to pitiless blankness and he shook his head. 'There is no us.'

Emma couldn't keep herself from giving one small gasp of pain. 'I don't know what that man told you...' she began but Larenzo didn't say anything. She drew in a ragged breath. 'You know what? It doesn't even matter. I don't care what Bertrano Raguso told you, because nothing makes what you've said to me justifiable. You say you don't trust people,' she continued, her voice shaking. 'Well, I trusted you, Larenzo, and I shouldn't have.' A muscle flickered in his jaw, but that was all the response she got. She felt like hitting him, hurting him, and so she did the only way she knew how. 'I hate you!' she spat. 'I hate you for making me care about you, and then doing this.' And with tears spilling down her cheeks, she snatched up Ava and stormed down the hall.

Alone in her bedroom, she sagged against the door. Ava squirmed to get down and Emma let her before sinking slowly to the floor, her knees drawn up to her chest. Her head was spinning, tears still trickling down her cheeks. How had it come to this so quickly, so terribly?

She felt as she had when Larenzo had been dragged off by the police. *She felt as she had when she'd left her mother's.*

The realisation was like a lightning streak of pain. She was acting just as she had then, storming away, refusing to engage. She didn't even remember what the argument with her mother had been about, the one that had set them both off and made Emma leave. She just remembered feeling furious and hurt and unloved, and instead of staying and battling it out she'd booked a ticket back to Berlin, where her father had been living at the time.

This time, did she possess the strength and courage not to walk away, but to stay and fight? Fight for herself, fight for Larenzo, fight for their family.

Walking away had been a way to protect herself, to pretend she wasn't hurt when she'd spent years aching inside. She wasn't going to make the same mistake now. She'd learned that much, at least.

Taking a deep breath, Emma rose from the floor. She picked up Ava, settling her on her hip, and then flung open her bedroom door and marched out into the living room.

The sight of Larenzo slouched in a chair, his head in his hands, made her insides twist with sorrow.

'I'm not,' she announced, 'going to let you do this.'

Larenzo looked up, his hair ruffled, his skin nearly grey with exhaustion. 'Excuse me?'

'I'm not going to let you destroy us, Larenzo. Whatever Bertrano told you, it's not worth it. I'm not going to let you throw away the happiness we've found together simply because some selfish old man is trying to ruin it for you and for us.' She took a deep breath and then ploughed on. 'I love you, you know. I'm not giving up. Not that easily. I gave up on my mother, when I was a teenager. Meghan helped me to see my part in the failure of our relationship. I'm not giving up on you.'

He stared at her for a long moment and then looked away without speaking. So it wasn't going to be easy. She couldn't say she was surprised.

'I want to show you something,' she said, and, setting Ava down on the floor, she marched over to the Christmas tree and retrieved a present from underneath it. She thrust it towards Larenzo; he took it, resting it in his lap, making no move to open it.

'It's my Christmas present to you,' Emma stated. 'Open it.'

He glanced up at her, and then, with a tiny shrug, he opened the present. The frame was made of silver, an elaborate twisting of ivy that Emma had liked because it was a live and growing thing, just as their relationship was. Their family was.

And the picture the frame held—it was of their family. It had been taken a few weeks ago at the playground. Emma had put the camera on a tripod and timer and run over to pose with Larenzo and Ava; their faces were all smooshed together, filled with laughter. It wasn't a candid moment, but it was close, and it was a picture that was filled with love and happiness. With joy.

Larenzo stared down at it for an endless moment. Emma held her breath as he traced their three faces with his fingers. Then he closed his eyes briefly and her heart gave a painful squeeze. 'Emma.'

'Larenzo,' she said softly, waiting.

He didn't speak for a long moment. Finally he said, 'Bertrano told me that he…he never cared for me. The only reason he'd ever approached me was to use me.' He looked up then, his face so unbearably bleak. 'So if things went wrong, he could blame it all on me. It's diabolical, really, to use a child that way. But he did and it worked.'

'Oh, Larenzo.' She stared at him helplessly; she could not imagine what hearing that must have felt like. A whole new and worse kind of grief.

'The thing is, I never even guessed. I never doubted, growing up, that he cared about me. Oh, I was suspicious at first, of course I was. But the more time he spent with me, the safer I felt… I really did think he loved me, like a son.' He shook his head slowly. 'Even when he betrayed me, I thought how it must have hurt him. How it must have been a hard decision to make. What a fool I am,' he spat, his voice thick with disgust. 'What a blind fool.'

'You're a person who, despite everything, believes the best of people. That's not a bad thing, Larenzo.'

'I took the blame because I loved him,' he said starkly. 'I could have fought it. I might have even won. But I didn't because I wanted to spare him. Spare the man who felt only contempt for me.' He looked away from her. 'It makes me feel sick.'

'But Bertrano is the sick one, Larenzo. Sick and sad and cruel to treat anyone, much less a child, that way. Don't blame yourself for his evil.' She took a step towards him, longing to touch him, to hold him, but afraid even now he might pull away. 'Don't let his evil taint what we have.'

The silence stretched on as Larenzo kept his face averted. Emma had no idea what he was thinking, but she felt instinctively that their whole lives hung in the balance of this moment.

'I thought I loved you,' he said finally. 'But I'm not sure any more I know what love is.'

'I know what love is,' Emma answered. 'Love is waking up in the night with Ava. Love is the three of us laughing around the dinner table. Love is turning over in bed and seeing you sleeping with a smile on your face that I know I put there. And,' she finished, her heart starting to pound, 'love is trusting that we'll keep going no matter what happens. We'll stay together and we'll battle it out. I won't walk away and neither will you, and neither of us will let the other try to.' She felt her lips tremble and she blinked the tears back. 'Please, Larenzo.'

'Dada!' Ava squealed, jerking them out of the intensity of the moment. Emma watched, her breath held, as her daughter toddled towards Larenzo, stumbling as she reached him so he caught her in his arms and brought her up to his chest. He closed his eyes, his lips brushing Ava's hair.

'I'm sorry,' he whispered. Everything in Emma protested until Larenzo opened his eyes and gazed at her with so much hunger and need and love she nearly swayed where she stood. 'I'm sorry for putting you through so much. I'm sorry for being so…imperfect.'

'We're all imperfect.'

'I'm sorry for hurting you.' He stood up, Ava still in his arms, and walked towards her. 'I love you, Emma. And I'm so thankful you stayed and fought for me. For us.'

'Me too,' she whispered, and then he was folding her in his arms, and even better he was kissing her, as Ava patted both their cheeks.

'Dada,' she crowed. 'Mama.'

'Family,' Larenzo said, and kissed Emma again.

EPILOGUE

One year later

'CAREFUL NOW!' LARENZO called as Emma mounted the stepladder. She threw him a teasing glance over her shoulder and took another step up, the star in her hand.

It was Christmas Eve, and she was putting the star on top of their tree. Outside the city was blanketed in snow, and only that morning they'd had a birthday party for Ava, with Meghan and Ryan and his new baby sister Ella coming into the city to celebrate.

It had been a wonderful, crazy year, full of excitement and joy. So much joy. Emma had finally submitted her photographs and had had her first exhibition in SoHo. In May the investigation had finally concluded and Larenzo's innocence had been proclaimed in all the papers. The gossip had trickled away, and Larenzo's business had gone from strength to strength, as he'd built his client list and invested in innovative new technology.

They'd moved from the luxurious penthouse apartment to a Brownstone overlooking the park, with bedrooms for the children they hoped one day to have. Ava was already obsessed with babies, and Emma was looking forward to introducing her to a new brother or sister, whenever it happened.

Now she stood on her tiptoes and perched the star on top of the tree.

'Is it straight?' she asked.

'Perfectly,' Larenzo answered.

'Star!' Ava crowed and, smiling at them both, Emma came down from the ladder.

She glanced at the star and then burst out laughing. 'It's completely crooked.'

'I like it,' Larenzo answered as he pulled her towards him, Ava squirming as usual to get right between them. 'It reminds me of how you love me despite my many imperfections.'

Emma shook her head, smiling. 'You seem pretty perfect to me,' she said, and kissed him.

* * * * *

MILLS & BOON®

The Rising Stars Collection!

This fabulous four-book collection features 3-in-1 stories from some of our talented writers who are the stars of the future! Feel the temperature rise this summer with our ultra-sexy and powerful heroes. Don't miss this great offer—buy the collection today to get one book free!

**Order yours at
www.millsandboon.co.uk/risingstars**